More Critical Pr:

for *Black*

• Selected for the Library Services for Youth in Custody 2015 In the Margins Book Award List
• One of *Library Journal*'s Best African American Fiction Books of 2014

"[A] heart-thumping thriller . . . K'wan does a masterful job of keeping readers on their toes right up to the very last page."
—*Publishers Weekly*

"Fans expecting another thug-in-the-street story will be pleasantly surprised at this rough police procedural."
—*Library Journal*

"Yet another heart-thumping thriller by this hip-hop author who delivers." —Library Services for Youth in Custody

"This book features the sublime story and character development that K'wan is known for." —*Urban Reviews*

for *Black Lotus 2: The Vow*

• Nominated for the 2021 Street Lit Writer of the Year Award

"*Black Lotus 2: The Vow* is full of the cinematic action and drama that K'wan is known for. Readers will be anxiously waiting for the next installment." —*Urban Reviews*

"K'wan delivers a lean, tightly plotted tale that balances noir aesthetics with comic book flair. Fans of pulp and urban lit will be well satisfied." —*Publishers Weekly*

THE RELUCTANT KING

THE RELUCTANT KING

BOOK 1: THE BOOK OF SHADOW

K'WAN

BROOKLYN, NEW YORK

This is a work of fiction. All names, characters, places, and incidents are a product of the author's imagination. Any resemblance to real events or persons, living or dead, is entirely coincidental.

Published by Akashic Books
©2021 K'wan

Hardcover ISBN: 978-1-63614-015-5
Paperback ISBN: 978-1-63614-014-8
Library of Congress Control Number: 2021935239

Crown vector art by happymeluv/vecteezy

Akashic Books
Brooklyn, New York
Twitter: @AkashicBooks
Facebook: AkashicBooks
E-mail: info@akashicbooks.com
Website: www.akashicbooks.com

THE KING FAMILY

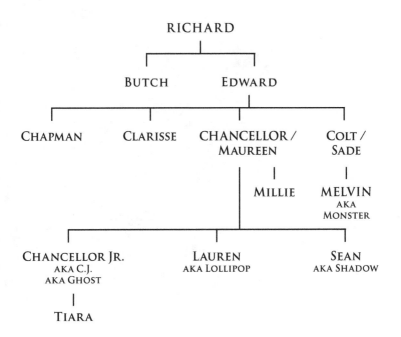

RICHARD

BUTCH   EDWARD

CHAPMAN   CLARISSE   CHANCELLOR /
MAUREEN   COLT /
SADE

MILLIE   MELVIN
AKA
MONSTER

CHANCELLOR JR.
AKA C.J.
AKA GHOST   LAUREN
AKA LOLLIPOP   SEAN
AKA SHADOW

TIARA

PROLOGUE

When Freddy rounded the corner of 138th, a gust of wind hit him in the chest, pushing his thin frame slightly left. He pulled his jacket tight around his neck, but it didn't do much good considering he was wearing a spring jacket despite it being early winter. Bitter winds scorched his skin, but Freddy ignored the frostbite that was trying to set in and instead focused on the small parcel in his pocket. He had less than a block to go and the sooner he made it the better.

It had been hours since Freddy's last fix, and he was starting to feel that itch on his back. He absently stroked the parcel in his pocket, making sure that it hadn't escaped during his walk from the drug spot. Freddy promised himself that it would be his last time—the same weak promise he had made a dozen times over the last few months, which always came right before he was about to blast off. In his heart, he always meant it, but once he was in the thralls of heroin, neither his word nor his integrity no longer meant much.

Freddy had once been a promising young hustler with heavy ties to the criminal underworld. On the road to doing big things, he'd somehow lost his way. It started out as a recreational thing, the occasional sprinkle of coke in his blunt to give it an extra kick. He soon graduated to snorting and formed a real love for cocaine. It allowed him to stay awake and party for days on end, last longer in bed as he threw dick like a porn star. For him, cocaine was the greatest thing since sliced bread, and he fell even more in love when he learned you could get a better blast if you cooked it. The standard coke high made him feel like a superhero, but crack made him a god.

In just six months he had managed to smoke up his jewelry, his car, and his self-respect. Crack had turned him into such a greaseball that no one would touch him with a ten-foot pole, not his street family nor his biological one. Word was out that he was bad news. Only a select few still had enough compassion in their hearts to risk throwing Freddy the occasional bone, but after he recently double-crossed one of them, he knew he'd soon have no one. Freddy wanted to feel bad about betraying one of the last people on earth still willing to look out for him, but he was an addict and addicts were without shame.

As Freddy walked down the block toward Adam Clayton Powell Jr. Boulevard, he couldn't help but notice how empty the streets were. The bad weather had sent most people indoors, but 138th was a hot block and there was almost always at least a few people outside. He'd been on the block for a while now and not even a car had come down the normally busy street. An eerie feeling crept over Freddy, and he hurried his pace.

For a second, he thought he heard footsteps behind him, but when he looked back he didn't see anyone. He chalked it up to the echo of his own boots slapping the concrete. But then he heard the footsteps again, and when Freddy stopped they continued on. He spared a glance over his shoulder and confirmed that he wasn't alone. Less than a half block behind him was a man dressed in a black hooded sweatshirt. It didn't take Freddy's junkie brain long to process what was about to go down.

He took off in a sprint down the street. If he made it to the next avenue, he'd be good. There'd be too many witnesses for the hooded man to commit his sinister intentions. Freddy ran with everything he had, wheezing and breathing heavy from his years of smoking cigarettes, yet he dared not stop. Soon, the busy street corner came into view. Against his better judgment he chanced a look back to gauge the distance between himself and the hooded man, but as he swerved his head around, he blindly ran into what felt like a brick wall and then crashed to the ground. Stars danced in his eyes. When Freddy peered up into the weak streetlight, he could barely make out the face hidden beneath the hood, though one look into those familiar, hateful eyes and Freddy knew they'd be the last things he ever saw.

"I didn't give them anything!" he shouted.

"Sure, you didn't, Fred. They picked my man's name out of a hat and decided at random to hang all that time on him." The hooded figure's voice dripped with sarcasm. "Your bullshit ensured two things. One is that there's a little boy out there who will likely never get to see his father outside of a prison visiting room. And two, the sanitation department is going to have to hose what's left of your scruples off this sidewalk."

Freddy opened his mouth, but the hooded man blew his brains out before he had the chance to speak again.

Though his victim was dead, the hooded man wasn't done. He wanted Freddy to serve as an example to all the others who thought they could violate him. He produced a pair of wire cutters from his pocket, ready to have a bit of fun, but then heard a gasp from somewhere above him. Perched near a second-floor window was a young boy of about nine or ten. When he saw that he'd been spotted, the boy froze, knowing that he would likely be the next to die for what he'd witnessed. The hooded man held the boy's gaze for a moment before raising a gloved hand to his lips and fading into the shadows.

A half hour passed before the police showed up. During

their canvass of the neighborhood, they questioned the little boy from the second floor. He was too frightened to speak at first, and when they grilled him about who had killed Freddy, he was only able to utter two words: "A ghost."

PART I

Born to Be Kings

CHAPTER 1

S hadow woke with a start. He sat bolt upright on his king-sized bed, gasping for air like a drowning man who had just broken the ocean's surface. The night terrors had returned.

For as long as he could remember, Shadow had been plagued with nightmares. Sometimes, when he closed his eyes, his brain was assaulted with violent flashes of events past, present, and possibly future. These dreams were sometimes so vivid that he would awake not knowing if he was still in his dreamworld or the real one, a point between sleep and consciousness that blurred the lines of reality just enough to where he questioned which side of his brain he was operating on. His mother had told him that he was born with a veil, a second sight of sorts, and that he should focus on deciphering the things he saw in his dreams rather than suppressing them. But she wasn't the one seeing her friends and loved ones, and sometimes herself, murdered every night. They weren't her nightmares.

The violent dreams caused Shadow to dodge sleep by any means necessary. Though he was only seventeen years old, sometimes he would stay up late drinking coffee and popping pills to keep himself from dozing off. When he became too restless, he slipped out of the house to hang out with his friends in the hood. It wasn't unusual to see Shadow lurking in some doorway in the middle of the night or silently passing over a block. Since childhood he'd been adept at moving silently, which was how he got his nickname.

The battle between Shadow and sleep deprivation had become a game. He sometimes went for days on end only taking catnaps. His longest sleepless stretch was seventy-two hours. The game was murder on his body, but it was also the ultimate test of will, resisting what came naturally. More often than not he fought the good fight, but his body could go without sleep for only so long. Eventually, his eyelids dropped like lead weights and his resistance ceased, sleep coming to collect him and deliver him back to his nightmares. His dreams weren't always bad. Most of the time he could handle them. Not recently, though. His nightmares had worsened ever since he started receiving visits from his deceased uncle, Colt.

A few years back, Shadow's dad, Chance, was diagnosed with cancer. Thankfully it wasn't terminal, but the chemo treatments did a number on his body and he was temporarily unable to perform the day-to-day operations of his business. During Chance's recovery, it fell to his youngest brother, Colt, to step up. Colt was a great leader who all men loved. He was also a strong surrogate father to Shadow and his siblings. Although he was close with all his nieces and nephews, Colt shared a special bond with Shadow. It wasn't necessarily that he loved Shadow more, it was just that Shadow required a bit more guidance than the rest. He didn't have C.J.'s cunning, Lolli's ruthlessness, or even Millie's heart, all qualities inherited from their parents. Shadow was a different sort. He wasn't soft, just set in his own ways.

Shadow spent a great deal of time with Uncle Colt, watching his every move. Colt was essentially his mentor and Shadow desperately wanted to be like him, yet he didn't have the stomach to do what his uncle did. Colt was a gangster and his deeds in the name of their family made him a feared man. He was the law in their little kingdom; his peacekeepers were a small, highly trained bunch who called themselves the Reapers. In the streets, the Reapers were hailed as some of the best at what they did—killing. Once set loose, the Reapers devoured their prey like wild dogs, but the hearts of their kills were always left for Colt. Shadow's uncle believed that separating the hearts from the bodies of his enemies prevented their souls from passing into the afterlife. For Colt, it wasn't enough that you suffered in life; he wanted you to suffer in death too. Rumor had it that he kept these hearts in jars, like trophies. Though Shadow had never seen his uncle's trophy collection, he knew enough not to doubt the rumors. He loved his uncle, and it broke his heart when he got the news that Colt was dead.

It happened around the time Chance had recovered enough to return to work and reclaim his seat at the head of the table. The police notified their family that Colt's body had been found inside his BMW at a rest stop somewhere in Delaware. The cause of death was a single gunshot to the head. According to the report, it was a robbery gone bad, though the story didn't sit right. Colt wore nearly twenty thousand dollars' worth of jewelry, which the robbers apparently overlooked. More disturbing was the fact that Colt was too cautious of a man to ever let a stranger get that close to him. This meant that he likely knew his killer.

When word of Colt's death got out, the streets screamed for justice, but no voices roared louder than those of the Reapers. They demanded blood. When it didn't come fast enough, they went out and sought it on their own. Their killing spree was so violent that people still talked about it. In the end, no one could say for sure if any of the poor souls they laid down in Colt's name had been responsible for his death. Eventually, the murders began to affect the family business and Chance had to step in. Though he was the boss, he had no real power over his brother's dogs. Short of risking a war with the Reapers, there wasn't much he could do to call them off. This was a problem Chance couldn't solve on his own, so he sought help from the only person who probably loved Colt more than he did—his widow.

The Reapers respected Sade. She wasn't just Colt's wife, she was one of them. Sade had put in work on the front lines so her word carried weight. The murders stopped, but resentments lingered. Colt had been the glue that bound the Reapers to the King family. When he died, so did the agreement the Reapers had with Chance.

Exactly one month after they laid Colt to rest, Shadow started receiving the visits. Colt arrived in his dreams not as the loving uncle who had taught him how to defend himself and properly apply condoms, but as something pulled from the deepest corners of his fears. The apparition would appear as an ashen corpse with eyes that burned of hellfire, the bullet wound in his temple still fresh and leaking blood. The creature silently followed Shadow through his nightmares, watching in anticipation until Shadow died. Because Shadow always perished in these dreams. Like clockwork, the moment before Shadow met his end, the creature would open its mouth to shout a warning that Shadow could never quite catch. The demonized version of his uncle was no doubt an omen of something to come, but Shadow couldn't figure out what that omen was.

As he rubbed his eyes awake, the smell of something delicious seeped into his room, snatching him from his reflective state. When the scent traveled from his nose to his stomach, his insides churned. He was starving. But when he tried to move his legs to get out of bed, he found them pinned. Jerking the covers back, he saw a sleeping doll whose limbs were intertwined with his. He couldn't remember her name, though he remembered her performance the night before, which brought a smile to his face and a warmth to his loins. As much as he would've liked another taste of her goodies, it was time for her to go.

"Wake up, shorty," Shadow said. He nudged her twice before she finally opened her sleepy brown eyes.

"Morning," she yawned. "What time is it?"

"Time to bounce," Shadow told her.

She smiled lazily and draped her arms around his neck. "Are we going to get some breakfast?"

"Nah, I got class this morning. I'll get at you later though." He pried free of her grip and slid out of bed, then grabbed his cell phone from the nightstand and moved to the dresser to select a pair of boxers.

She frowned. "Okay, well, can you at least drop me off on your way to school?"

"I already called you an Uber. It should be outside by the time you finish getting dressed. Just do me a favor and take the back door on your way out."

"You sure know to make a girl feel good."

"I'm a King, that's what we do," he replied. "Dig, I'm about to shower so I can start my day. If you get any larcenous ideas, keep in mind that every room in the house is monitored by cameras."

As he shuffled to the bathroom, an afterthought popped into his head. Over his shoulder he said, "Oh, and take her with you."

As if on cue, a second girl emerged from the sheets. This one was blond and thin, with fake breasts. Her blue eyes were heavy with sleep. She tussled her hair and said, "What'd I miss?"

The hot shower helped to clear the fog that had settled into Shadow's head. He was no fan of tequila, but this hadn't stopped him from having eight shots of it the night before. He and some of his gang had gotten together to commemorate the passing of one of his best friends. It had been one year to the day since Lou had his young life snuffed out. Unlike some of his other friends, Lou wasn't a street kid. He came from a two-parent home, got good grades, and treated everyone he met with respect. Lou was a good dude whose only crime was associating with the wrong crowd—namely Shadow. Had Lou not been hanging out in a project apartment with Shadow that day, he would've never been hit by a stray bullet. The saddest part was that the boy who killed him hadn't even been shooting at Lou. He was shooting his pistol in the air for the hell of it and one of the bullets took a wrong turn through the window Lou was sitting next to. Though Shadow wasn't directly responsible for what happened to Lou, he still carried the guilt from it.

Shadow wiped away the steam from the bathroom mirror and stared at himself. He was an athletically built young man with skin the color of midnight and thick black hair that he wore in cornrows. He was beginning to sprout hair on his chin too, but it was taking its time growing in. Shadow was a hand-some devil, though it had taken him years to realize it. Of all his father's children, he was the only one who hadn't inherited his fair skin. He was even darker than his mother, who had a smooth brown complexion. Being the darkest one in the house sometimes made him feel like an outsider. His mother had al-ways reinforced that his black was beautiful and that him being darker than the others was what made him unique. But Shadow didn't want to be unique, he wanted to look like everyone else. It wasn't until he was older that he learned to be comfortable in his skin, but he still had his moments of low self-esteem. Though he'd never admit to it, his insecurities were part of why he dogged women the way he did.

Shadow came out of the bathroom and wasn't surprised to find the women gone. They were likely pissed at how he'd given them the boot, but they'd get over it. Even if they didn't, what was it to him? There was no shortage of women who would eagerly occupy his bed and consider it an honor. After all, he was royalty.

Once he finished dressing, he inspected himself in the mirror. His cashmere sweater was crisp, and the cuffs of his black jeans fell over his suede Timberlands just the way he wanted them too. A few spritzes of cologne and he deemed himself presentable enough to join his family for breakfast.

CHAPTER 2

Maureen King stood over the stovetop, scrambling eggs in a T-Fal pan. Using a ball of paper towels, she dabbed at a bit of sweat forming above her brow. It was hot in the kitchen and she hoped her hair would hold up under the silk scarf tied around her head as she finished working her magic. Normally breakfast would've been prepared by their housekeeper, Mrs. Norma, while Maureen slept. This morning, though, was different. It was an important day and she needed to dictate how it went from start to finish.

After giving the eggs one last whip, she hustled over to the stainless steel refrigerator to grab the carafe of orange juice, which she had spent a good portion of the morning squeezing. She untied her silk robe and shuffled the heels of her plush slippers across the linoleum floor. Maureen was a diva at all times, even in her night clothes. She paused to examine her reflection in the refrigerator door. Even though she was in her early forties, you'd believe it if she told you she was younger. Her skin was a high-yellow shade and her eyes were a brilliant hazel. When she puckered her lips, they looked like tangerine slices. She couldn't help but smile at the vintage beauty staring back at her. She took good care of herself and always had. Maureen was a queen and wore her crown well.

Twenty-five years ago, if someone had told Maureen she would go from living in a roach-infested tenement in Harlem to a 3,300-square-foot home in Englewood Cliffs, New Jersey, she'd have laughed in their face. Little girls from the ghetto don't get happy endings, or so her mother used to say. Maureen's journey argued against such wisdom. She was a street chick–turned-housewife, and her road to the throne was anything but well-paved. A drunk and part-time heroin addict, Maureen's mother couldn't keep her shit together long enough to make sure she ate dinner. Her father was slightly better but he didn't stick around long enough to add to Maureen's suffering. Life had been unkind to her, but she refused to accept what it dished her way. As a kid, when things got really bad, she learned to shut off part of her brain and transport herself into a fantasy land where she reigned as queen. It was her only escape from the pain, and the vision that drove her to making her imagined life a reality.

The time for fantasies ended when she got pregnant at sixteen. Upon learning that her baby was a girl, she chose to name her Millicent, after her grandmother—Millie for short. Maureen had no maternal skills to speak of and no support from the man who impregnated her, but after Millie was born she managed to keep them both alive and fed. Having an extra mouth to feed only made Maureen want to more quickly actualize her dreams of queendom. To stay above the poverty line she did things she wasn't proud of, but it was her and her baby girl against the world. This all changed, of course, when Chancellor King entered her life.

The circumstances under which Chance and Maureen met were just as unconventional as their twenty-six years of marriage. A man by the name of Roth was making a run at the district attorney's office, and one night he threw an exclusive campaign party at a high-end Manhattan hotel. Socialites and power players from around the city gathered in a swanky ballroom, and Maureen found herself standing in the center of many important people. This was thanks to a well-to-do older gentleman she had been keeping time with back then. He'd brought Maureen with him as a showpiece to bolster his status, but it turned out that she was the one who received the boost.

That night she laid eyes on Chancellor King, who everyone referred to as Chance. She remembered seeing him amble across the room, dressed in a well-cut black suit, shaking hands and smiling like he belonged among the elite. His eyes, however, told a different story. They were the eyes of a man who had seen things in life that no one else in the room had . . . except for Maureen. A quiet inquiry revealed that Chance was there as the guest of a real estate tycoon who had contributed to Roth's campaign. Apparently, Chance was his protégé. Back then, Chance still rode the bench, flipping slum houses for a few thousand dollars' profit, but he'd yet to be officially subbed into the game. While the bigwigs focused on properties in Manhattan and downtown Brooklyn, Chance operated in the trenches. His first few property flips were dilapidated buildings in Brooklyn slums that no one else cared to deal with. On paper, the properties were a waste, but Chance was hopeful they'd become something worthwhile. In addition to Brooklyn, Chance was involved in an investment group that focused on an area of the city called Five Points. Although he served as the low man in these negotiations, he soon established himself as a major player, proving to be an excellent property buyer and seller. But real estate wasn't his real gift. Politics was where he shined.

That night at the hotel, a mutual associate introduced Chance and Maureen. Over a glass of expensive wine and dry conversation, their eyes spoke more than their mouths, detailing an instant spark. Once they moved past small talk and flirtation, they exchanged their life stories. It was as if they had been destined to meet that night.

Although Chance was a little older than Maureen, he had a boyish charm that didn't make her feel like she was being pressed by a dirty old man. Chance spent half the night watching her. She knew that when the evening wound down he would make his move, and he didn't disappoint. As he left, surrounded by members of his investment group, he slipped a business card into Maureen's hand and whispered, "Give me a call when you get tired of renting."

Three weeks passed before she called him. It wasn't for lack of wanting to; she was intrigued and wanted to get to know Chance, but she was hesitant. He was a rising star who appeared to be on his way to achieving great things, while she was a single mother stuck in the projects and living hand to mouth. Maureen feared that her baggage might scare him off. But to her surprise, Chance proved to be not only accepting of her situation but also of her daughter, Millie. In the following months, Maureen got to know who Chancellor King really was.

The Kings had been players in the New York underworld since the 1930s, starting with Chance's grandfather, Richard King. Richard made his bones smuggling booze for the Mafia during prohibition. He made even better money by skimming off the shipments and selling the extras in Black neighborhoods. He was making a killing from this side hustle until the mob made a killing of him.

The next to hold the reins of power was Edward King, Chance's father. He and his brother Butch monopolized the market during the heroin epidemic, which ran rampant through American ghettos after the Vietnam War. The brothers became very rich very quickly, yet they also had two very different ideas about how to spread their newfound wealth. Butch spent his money on material things like cars, jewelry, and women. Soon enough, he was one of the biggest hustlers in town. Meanwhile, Edward lived modestly, investing in properties and opening businesses. At the end of their run, Butch found himself doing thirty years in prison, while Edward had laid the foundation for something his children could build upon.

When it was Chance's turn to sit at the head of the table, he had a different vision for what the King family would become. The mistakes of his grandfather and uncle had shown him that the only real way to secure the King legacy was to legitimize some or all of it. And thus began his reign and his mission.

Things progressed quickly for Chance and Maureen. In a little over a year, she took his last name and gave him his first child, Chancellor Jr., who went by Ghost when he got older. Maureen proved herself not only to be a good wife and mother but also a valuable consigliere during troubled times, of which, in those first few years together, they had had more than their fair share. But Maureen's polish and drive inspired Chance to move deeper into power circles; her cunning helped him fortify his position on the streets. In one way or another, Maureen had orchestrated the events that led Chance to believing that he was a king in more than just name. It was her idea to establish a monarchy.

For as long as anyone could remember, the different ethnic groups that occupied Five Points had been at odds—until Chance stepped in. Thanks to a complex plan that Maureen helped put together, Chance accomplished something that hadn't been done in more than one hundred years: bringing the heads of all the major crime factions in Five Points together at one table. It was she who subtly suggested that Chance combine his criminal and political connections and use them to offer each organization something they wanted but couldn't obtain. It was like a grab bag of earned favors. Chance had

something to offer everyone that they couldn't refuse. To ice
the cake, Maureen began whispering into the ears of the wives
and girlfriends who would sit at the table. They used their influence over their lovers to push them toward Maureen's goals.
When the group of gangsters unanimously elected Chance to
serve as the chairman of their new collective, it was he who received the pats on the back, but Maureen was the one who had
made it all possible. She was a sweetheart, but she could be a
cold-blooded snake, something that made her far more dangerous than Chance. The criminal empire she had inherited might
not have been the fairy-tale kingdom she had once dreamed
about, but she sat on a throne nonetheless.

With Chance's star rising, and his hold over his criminal
enterprises now solidified, Maureen persuaded him to set his
sights on a much bigger game than the one they had been playing in Five Points. She wasn't content with a slice of the pie.
She wanted the whole thing.

"Happy birthday, Ma!" Shadow said, startling Maureen when
he came walking through the swinging kitchen doors. He am-
bled over to his mother and planted a kiss on her cheek.

"Thank you, Sean," Maureen replied, calling him by his
given name. "It must be snowing in hell if you're the first one
down for breakfast."

"Ma, if I didn't know any better, I'd think you were trying
to call me lazy." Shadow plucked a piece of bacon from the
platter on the table, not realizing how hot it was until it burned
his fingers, causing him to drop it back onto the platter.

"I'm not calling you lazy," Maureen said, picking up the
now slightly cooler piece of bacon and popping it in her mouth.
"You just aren't the most motivated of all my children." She
added honey to the breakfast biscuits. "I take it you must've

had quite a wild night if you forgot my rule. What's my rule, Sean?"

Shadow looked at the floor. He had hoped to avoid one of his mother's speeches, but it didn't look like he'd have that kind of luck this morning.

"Let me help you out," Maureen continued. "Get them vampire bitches in after dusk and out before dawn. The last thing I wanna see on the wake-up is one of your skeezers."

"I'm sorry, Ma. I was going to send them home last night, but I fell asleep."

"And that's your problem, Sean. You're always sleeping and need to wake your ass up. This home is our sanctuary, the place where all my Kings, and the princess, rest their heads, which makes it a sacred place. That being said, I shouldn't have to constantly remind you that we take the trash out, not bring it in. You're royalty, and you need to start acting like a prince instead of the damn joker. How can you be trusted to help carry your father's legacy if you're looked at as irresponsible?"

Shadow sucked his teeth. "Come on, Ma. We all know who Daddy is grooming for the big chair. I'm not even in the running. That's been made clear to me."

"Don't act like you're being slighted because C.J. is next up. He's the oldest male, so by right it goes to him. It's been that way for almost a hundred years."

Shadow rolled his eyes. "I know, *tradition*. I'm cool with that, Ma. Ghost is more than welcome to the headaches that come with being king." It was true: Shadow had little stomach for the family business.

"Do you hear yourself? *Ghost is more than welcome to the headaches of being king*," Maureen said. "Spoken like a true sucker and not one of my boys. We were Kings long before your daddy took his seat at the head of the table. We are of noble blood and are expected to carry ourselves accordingly. Don't matter which King sits in the big chair, what matters is that every King can be depended on to hold what we got. Every one of you I pushed out of my crotch is here for a purpose, and that's to help make sure we stay on top. You need to get your head out of your ass and get with the program."

Shadow took his customary seat at the foot of the breakfast table and muttered, "Whatever you say, Ma."

"I need you to run uptown for me today," Maureen told him while dumping eggs into a serving dish.

"No problem. I'll go as soon as I get out of school."

"School can wait. This can't."

"If you're cosigning me cutting school then this must be important. What do you need me to go get?"

"Not what . . . *who*," she said. "I hear Millie's been hanging around the projects. I need you to go and see if you can track her down for me."

Shadow's face darkened. "Not this shit again. Ma, why do you even bother stressing yourself out over that girl?"

"Watch your mouth!" Maureen spat. "And *that girl* is still just as much my child as your Black ass is."

Millie was a sensitive subject in the King household. She was Shadow's half sister and Maureen's firstborn. Of all the King children, Shadow and Millie had the most turbulent relationship. She constantly picked on him when they were younger about being darker than the rest of them and would often make him cry by calling him cruel names like Tar Baby and Monkey Boy. Shadow was relieved the first time Millie ran away from home, but unfortunately, she returned. Unlike Shadow and the others, who had been born into privilege, Millie came up rough and wore her emotional scars on her sleeve. Chance always treated Millie like she was one of his and provided her with all the same comforts as he did his biological children, but it never seemed to be enough. She was a rebel who refused to play by anyone's rules but her own. Things only grew worse when she got hooked on drugs.

Chance and Maureen tried everything, from putting Millie in overpriced rehab facilities to threatening to cut her off, but Millie just couldn't stay straight. The last time she stayed under the King roof she had stolen some of her mother's jewelry and one of Chance's cars. Chance washed his hands of her after that but Maureen still held onto hope that one day her daughter would get her act together.

"Sean," Maureen went on, "I know things ain't never been easy between you and Millie, but try to understand that not everything she's said or done has been her fault. Drugs change people . . . take them out of their right state of mind. Millie can be foul, but she's sick. It's up to us as her family to try and help her get well."

"Okay, Ma," Shadow responded, "I'll go hit the hood and find out if anybody has seen her."

"Thank you, Sean." Maureen kissed her son on the forehead. "I know you don't want to, but in this life we have chosen to live, we sometimes find ourselves doing things we don't agree with. It's all a part of being a King, putting the good of the family above what you feel is right or wrong. Do you understand?"

"Yes, Ma."

Maureen wiped her hands on a dish towel. "Now, this little mission I'm sending you on has to stay between us. I don't want your father to know what's going on and I sure as hell don't want you to tell C.J."

"Tell me what?" the elder son said as he entered the kitchen through the back door. He was decked out in a tailored blue suit that hugged his wide frame. Beneath his jacket he wore a salmon-colored shirt and a blue necktie. The two brothers favored each other, but unlike Shadow, who was borderline *pretty*, C.J. was ruggedly handsome, with fair skin and a square jaw covered in fine black stubble. He looked from his mother to his brother and back again, waiting for an answer.

"Nothing, it's just that Sean got in trouble in school again," Maureen lied.

C.J. popped Shadow on the back of the head. "What the hell is wrong with you? How many times do I gotta tell you how important education is?"

Shadow rubbed his scalp where his brother had hit him. "It wasn't that big of a deal, so I don't know why you're tripping, Ghost." The only people who still called him C.J. or Chancellor Jr. were their mother and his fiancée—at least when she wanted to get on his nerves.

Ghost slammed one of his thick palms on the table hard enough to rattle the silverware. "I'm tripping because we've invested too much money on your education for you to fuck it up and end up like one of the dead-end knuckleheads you hang out with!"

"Junior!" Maureen said.

The sound of his mother's voice always had a calming effect on Ghost. "Shadow," he said in a softer tone, "I know when I ride you about school you think I'm being a dick, but all I'm trying to do is make sure you are afforded every opportunity to be great. An educated man is a man with options."

"I've got plenty of options, Ghost. Not only is Daddy one of the most successful Realtors in the tristate, but he's also got money coming in from two dozen dope houses around the city—and those are just the ones I know about. Don't even get me started on the gambling and girls! By hook or by crook, I've got options."

Ghost's eyes flashed with anger. "First of all, watch your

damn mouth. You know we don't talk that talk in the house. And second, it's obvious from your dumbass statement that you don't know the difference between controlling and owning." He shook his head. "And you wonder why I'm always up your ass about school? This little monarchy we've established within Five Points only exists because the arrangement is lucrative for all parties involved. It's the collective controlling factions in the Points who back our father that make him a respected player all over the city, not just in the Points. This is a grand old house that Chancellor King has built, but never forget that houses get torn down every day."

"Not this house. We're built Ford tough," Shadow said.

"I'm sure they said the same thing about the World Trade Center right before 9/11," Ghost shot back. "You're young and can't see far enough past your need to have a good time to understand that the world isn't all about jewelry, cars, and women. That's short-term shit. You have to think about things in terms of where you see yourself ten to fifteen years from now. Why do you think Dad says he'll cut off any one of us who doesn't graduate college? In the event that this all goes sour one day, each of us has to be able to stand on his own to carry this legacy or create new ones."

"I hear you, Ghost," Shadow said half-heartedly.

Ghost grabbed his brother by the back of his neck and gave a little squeeze. "Don't just hear me, little brother—*listen* to me."

"Okay, that's enough business talk at the table," Maureen cut in, setting one of the serving dishes down on a place mat.

"Sorry, Mama," Ghost said. "I'm just trying to give lil' bro some game." Ghost rubbed the top of Shadow's head affectionately. "We good?" He extended his fist.

Shadow stared at it for a moment, faking hurt, before smiling and pounding Ghost's fist. "Fo' sho'."

Ghost could be a pain in the ass, but he was still one of Shadow's heroes. Growing up, their father spent most of his time working to ensure that the family had everything they needed, so Ghost shouldered a lot of the man-of-the-house responsibilities. Besides Colt, Ghost was the closest thing Shadow had to a mentor. And though you couldn't tell from the suit he wore that morning, Ghost was a gangster—a pure street nigga. He had inherited Uncle Colt's violent temper and disregard for human life, which was how he earned the nickname Ghost. Men who ran afoul of him left the world of the living.

Unlike Shadow, who their parents kept away from that side of the business, Ghost was pulled in headfirst. It wasn't that their parents wanted Ghost to get into the life; there just wasn't much they could've done to stop it. Ghost had come into the world street-poisoned. Murder and mayhem were in his heart, and once it became clear to Chance that he couldn't do anything to suppress his oldest son's natural instincts, he started doing what he could to sharpen them. Reluctantly, he schooled his namesake on the ins and outs of the family's *other* business. Ghost took to crime like a fish to water. In the early days, Chance kept his eager son on a short leash, but once he was deemed ready, the shackle was removed and Ghost proved his bite far worse than his bark. While Chance closed deals in boardrooms, his firstborn closed caskets in the hood. Ghost emerged as a modern-day Al Capone, but then something happened that shifted his interests—he became a father.

Having his daughter, Tiara, put things in perspective for Ghost. His new focus became being a good dad and providing the best life for his little girl. Ghost came in off the streets and tried his hand at earning a legitimate income. He drew a nice monthly check from his position on the board of Second Chance Developers, but he also ran a towing and salvage company. Driving trucks wasn't the most glamorous job, but it ensured he'd return home safe to his lady and his daughter every night. Officially, Ghost was retired from the family's dirty business, but stories had been floating around that contradicted this myth.

"Oh, I almost forgot," Ghost said, shooting up out of his chair and planting a kiss on his mother's cheek.

"I was wondering if I was going to have to remind you," Maureen said with a smile.

Ghost reached into his back pocket and removed an envelope, which he handed to her. "You know I'd never forget my favorite gal's special day."

Maureen held the envelope in both hands. "Feels a little light to be cash."

"You got plenty of that, Mama. And I don't shop for what people want—I shop for what they need."

Maureen opened the envelope and withdrew a laminated postcard with an itinerary printed on it. She wasn't quite sure what to make of it.

"That there is the golden ticket for you and three of your friends to go out and play like you're young again," Ghost said proudly. "It starts with brunch at that place you like in Philly, followed by a full treatment at the spa, and, finally, two hours at the gun range. Just don't tell Daddy about that last part."

"Aw, thank you so much, C.J.," Maureen said, fighting back tears.

"It's hard to shop for the woman who has everything, so I'm glad I was able to make you smile," he said. "So, what'd Shadow get you?"

Shadow could've kicked his brother for the shade he'd just thrown, but he kept his game face. "I gotta go and pick it up. I'm gonna give it to her at the party tonight." In truth, Shadow had been so caught up with his own bullshit that he hadn't remembered it was his mother's birthday until he woke up that morning. He would have to grab something for her when he went into the city to look for Millie.

"Don't worry, baby. I'm sure your gift will be just as thoughtful as your brother's." Maureen knew Shadow was lying.

"So, where are you off to this morning dressed all fancy?" Shadow asked Ghost, glad to change the subject. Usually, at this hour, Ghost would be dressed in coveralls and work boots, getting ready to head to the salvage yard.

"I got a meeting this morning. Some guy is giving Christian grief about this building we're supposed to be leasing to open a nightclub. I'm going to go have a *chat* with him."

"Big bro, you about to own a club? Good, now I don't have to worry about ID when I wanna go out for drinks!"

"Slow your drunk-ass down. It isn't my club. I'm a silent investor. This will be Christian's baby to run as he sees fit. I'm just helping out."

Maureen snorted. "That one."

"Knock it off, Mama," Ghost said. "Christian and his little crew have brought a lot of money into this family over the years. He's been a loyal soldier and I think it's long overdue that I help broaden his horizons."

"So long as they don't get too broad. I see plenty of ambition behind those painted eyes of his."

"Yes, Christian is ambitious as hell. If he wasn't, I wouldn't have taken him under my wing. *Never trust a man who's content to eat out of your hand forever.*"

"Spoken like your father," Maureen said, patting Ghost's cheek. "You'll make a fine king one day because you understand the importance of taking care of those who are loyal to you." She cut her eyes to Shadow. "Not even five minutes ago

I was stressing to Sean how it's important for us to look after our own."

"It's like you always taught us: we're all we got," Ghost said. He then took his usual seat, which was just to the right of the head of the table.

"Where's Dad?" Shadow asked. "I'm ready to eat." As per tradition, they wouldn't usually commence the meal until their father was seated.

"He had to leave a little earlier than usual today," Ghost said. "He's meeting with some *friends* of ours this morning."

"Dad is holding court this afternoon?" Shadow said, perking up. "I should be there."

"No, you shouldn't," Ghost replied.

A disappointed expression crossed Shadow's face. "C'mon, man. You and Lolli get to sit in when Dad holds court, so why can't I? I'm a King too!"

"Yes, but you're also still a kid, Shadow," Ghost said. "Why don't you enjoy your youth for a while before you rush off to try and shoulder grown folks' responsibilities? Besides, you're the one always hollering about how you don't want any part of the family business, right?"

"Sitting at the table isn't the same as sitting on the front line," Shadow countered.

"Isn't it?" Ghost said, raising an eyebrow. "Some of those old-timers at those tables are ten times as dangerous as any three fools running around with pistols. If a man approaches you with a gun, at least you can see that coming. Can't say the same thing about a double cross. You never see those coming and it's almost always the last person you expect. To sit at that table, you have to be able to see five steps ahead of your opponent, and even then, there's no guarantee you'll be able to do jack shit about what's coming."

"Contrary to what you might think, Ghost, your brother ain't no square," Shadow said.

"No, you ain't no square, but you ain't no beast either. And it's beasts that sit in those rooms."

"Even Daddy?"

"*Especially* Daddy," Ghost muttered.

"Maybe Sean is right, C.J.," Maureen chimed in. "Being around you and your daddy at court may help build his character."

"There is nothing wrong with Shadow's character, Mama," Ghost said.

"The hell there ain't," she said. "All that boy wants to do is play video games and chase tail. He needs to get a taste of how the real world operates. Maybe seeing his baby boy there will bring your father back to his senses and he'll rethink the three generations of work he's about to undo."

Shadow flashed his mother a dirty look. "What's that supposed to mean?"

"Nothing," Ghost said.

Shadow wanted to press the issue but Uncle Chapman disrupted the conversation, busting into the kitchen. He wore a blue silk bathrobe with a matching blue silk scarf tied around his head to hold his processed hair in place. The outfit made him look like an old R&B crooner displaced from the sixties. Chapman was Chance's older brother, and one of a set of twins. Whereas Chance was a kind and honest man, his brother and sister were cruel and sneaky. Because their last names were King, they carried themselves with a sense of entitlement for something neither of them had helped to build. This held especially true for Chapman. He felt slighted about Edward passing control of the family holdings to Chance instead of him, the eldest son, as had been the tradition of the King family for generations. No one in the house particularly

cared for Chapman and his sister Clarisse, but they were toler-
ated because they were Kings.

Without bothering to say good morning, Chapman sat
down at the breakfast table and started heaping food onto an
empty plate. This earned him a hard whack on the hand from
Maureen's spatula.

"For as long as you've been living in my house you'd think
you'd remember how things work, Chapman," Maureen
snapped.

"My brother's house," Chapman replied. "Cut me some
slack, Maureen. I've had a rough night and I'm not up for your
mothering this morning. Besides, isn't it your birthday? I'd
think you'd be glowing."

"I should be, but unfortunately I've gotta make sure everyone else is doing what they need to be doing before I can focus
on myself. After I finish feeding the troops I've got to catch my
hair appointment and then meet the party planner to go over a
few last-minute things."

"Mama, if it's your party, why is it up to you to do everything?"
Shadow asked. He knew his mother couldn't help trying to be
all things to all of them, but he didn't like the stress it put on her.

"That's the price of being the backbone of this family,"
Chapman told his nephew.

"That reminds me—did you remember to pick up your tuxedo from the tailor's yesterday, Sean?" Maureen asked.

"I forgot," Shadow said.

"Jesus, boy! Do I have to pin a note to your chest to get you
to remember the smallest things?"

"Relax, Ma. I'll pick it up this afternoon. I don't see why I
can't just wear one of the suits hanging in my closet."

"Because she wants you to look good when you meet your
intended," Chapman interjected.

"She's not my *intended* anything," Shadow said. "Just some stupid girl Daddy insists on me being nice to because he wants to do business with her uncle. It's not a big deal."

Chapman choked out a laugh. "My poor, naïve nephew. One of these days I'll have to sit you down and share a bit of family history with you."

"What are you talking about?" Shadow asked.

"Nothing, bro. Chapman is just flapping his dick suckers again," Ghost snarled.

Chapman swerved his eyes to his oldest nephew and bestowed a menacing glare, daring Ghost to sling another insult so he could at last reveal the secret, which was the source of Ghost's greatest shame. It was the one time he had broken his word with his family and it almost prompted a bloody feud. Chapman started to spill the beans just to be spiteful, but thought better of provoking Ghost and shut his mouth. The last time he'd gotten into it with his nephew, Ghost whipped him so bad that Chapman had to wear sunglasses for almost two weeks.

"So, where is my brother this morning?" Chapman said, changing the subject.

"Court," Shadow said.

This took Chapman by surprise. Ghost was Chance's right hand, but Chapman was his left. When dealing with important Five Points business, at least one of them was usually there to assist the king. Chapman frowned and glared at Ghost. "Why wasn't I made aware that we're holding court this morning?"

"Because it isn't an official gathering," Ghost said. "Just some stuff Daddy needs to take care of."

"That still doesn't explain why I wasn't notified," Chapman pressed.

"Maybe because you're the king's older brother and not the king," Maureen said with an edge.

"A mere oversight and an easy fix," Chapman said.

"Need I remind you of the punishment for treason in this monarchy, Uncle?" Ghost said, his voice flat and cold.

"Jesus, Ghost. Always so serious. Why don't you lighten up? You know I love my brother more than anything."

"I also know that if my father had no sons, you'd be next in line for his chair. So you can understand why you saying something like that could raise my eyebrows, don't you, Uncle?"

"The consummate guard dog," Chapman said, grinning. "You know, you remind me a lot of Colt. He too was overprotective of your father. In the end, the reward never justified the risk."

Maureen noticed Ghost's fist tighten around his fork. "Chapman," she said, "why don't you close that slick mouth of yours? Not everyone shares your twisted sense of humor."

"You're right, Maureen," Chapman said, nodding. "Sometimes I do play too much. You know I was joking, don't you, Ghost?"

Ghost didn't answer; instead, he busied himself trying to straighten the fork he had just bent.

"Since Chance has called this impromptu meeting, does that mean he's really going through with this foolish plan?" Chapman said.

"What plan?" Shadow asked.

Before Maureen or Ghost could respond, Chapman said, "You haven't heard? Your father is planning to relinquish his crown so he can make a run for president."

"Of the United States?"

Chapman rolled his eyes. "No, my dimwitted nephew. Of the borough."

Shadow looked to Ghost. "I don't understand."

"Dad is restructuring the organization to put a bit of distance between him and our illegal activities, so he's ready for his next big move."

"But he's maintained his position on the city council and as king of Five Points for years without the two overlapping," Shadow said. "Why do things have to change now?"

Ghost sighed, then caved. "Because the bigger the office, the bigger the spotlight. City council is little more than a fancy title—there isn't a whole lot of responsibility that comes with that and it allows Dad to serve two masters, so to speak. If Dad gets elected as Brooklyn's borough president, that will place him just a few chairs shy of mayor and thrust him into the spotlight, which means that we will be on the radar of just about every government agency you can imagine, including the FBI and DEA. He'll have to be squeaky clean. If your Uncle Chapman spent as much time involved in the family business as he does spending the family's money, he'd know this."

"So what does that mean for us? For Five Points?" Shadow asked.

"We go back to being everyday citizens," Chapman said smugly.

"Pay this idiot no mind, Shadow," Ghost said. "Things are definitely going to change in the near future, but for as long as there is a surviving member of the King family, one of us will always sit on the throne of Five Points."

"C'mon, y'all, the food is getting cold," Maureen interjected. "Call Lolli down so we can eat."

"Lolli's here?" Ghost asked. Since his sister moved into her own condo in Manhattan, they hardly saw her anymore.

"Showed up late last night drunk as a skunk and smelling like sin. She wanted to go home, but I made her go sleep it off in her room. She's probably still up there, passed out."

"I didn't see her in her room earlier," Shadow said. "The

door was open and the bed was made, which means she probably didn't sleep in it. You know Lollipop don't make no beds."

"Our paths crossed in the wee hours of the morning," Chapman informed them. "She was going out as I was coming in. She said she had to get an early jump on a piece of business."

Chapman knowing Lolli's comings and goings struck Shadow as odd. His sister, like most of them, didn't trust her uncle very much and would never let him in on her activities unless they were scheming on something together.

"And what business could that girl have today that's more important than having breakfast with her mama on her birthday?" Maureen asked Chapman, who just shrugged. "All that girl thinks about is money and boys."

"Just like Uncle Chapman," Ghost murmured, paying no mind to his uncle's sharp glare.

"That girl is determined to worry me to death," Maureen said. She worried about Lolli more than any of her children, and with good reason. Lolli had all of Millie's wild ways and curiosities about the streets but none of Millie's weaknesses. Lolli had a dominant personality that made her impossible to persuade; she did only what she wanted and God help the person who tried to force her to do otherwise. Lolli was a control freak—it was her way or no way. Maureen's heaviest concern about her youngest daughter, though, was that she liked to play dangerous games. Lolli seemed to get a thrill from putting herself in harm's way.

Ghost reached out and patted his mother's hand. "I wouldn't worry too much, Mom. That girl is probably better at taking care of herself than any of us. Besides, I'm pretty sure wherever she is, her shadow Nefertiti isn't too far behind. You know how protective she is of Lolli."

"A little *too* protective, if you ask me . . ." Shadow started to say more, but a look from Ghost silenced him.

"You focus on running the household and let me worry about Lauren," Ghost told his mother. "Lolli is probably just off somewhere being Lolli."

CHAPTER 3

"Damn, this pussy is so good," Mike panted, stroking away behind the shapely ass hiked up in front of him. Each time his penis went in and out of her wet pussy, it took him to a different level of pleasure.

"Prove it to me!" she commanded, slapping herself on the ass, making it jiggle. "Beat this pussy like it's the last time you're ever gonna get it!"

While Mike plowed into her like he was drilling for oil, Lolli looked on through the headboard mirror as if she was watching porn. Her long black hair spilled over her face, which was drenched with sweat. Every time Mike collided into her, she bit down on her bottom lip hard enough to draw blood. His strong hands moved up and down her tattooed back, making Lolli tingle. Yeah, Mike was giving her the business, but she'd never admit it.

"I'm about to bust," Mike whimpered. "I'm about to bust!" He grabbed her hips and thrust even faster.

"Uh-uh," Lolli said, sliding herself off his dick. She grabbed him by one arm and pulled him down on the bed, rolled him over onto his back, and mounted him. "You don't get yours until I get mine."

Mike was long; whenever he hit her walls she felt it in her stomach. Lolli didn't complain, though, she was a sucker for a good hurt. She adjusted herself until she found a comfortable position and went for what she knew. Every time she swirled her hips she could see Mike's face twist. She knew he wouldn't last much longer.

"Shit . . . shit . . . shit . . ." Mike chanted as Lolli put it on him. He felt his dick hit her wall and then a secret compartment somewhere in the back of her vagina opened up, letting him in deeper.

"That's right, get all the way in there," Lolli whispered. Waves of pleasure rode through her body every time the tip of Mike's dick hit her spot. She wanted to cry out but her breath caught in her throat, making it near impossible for her to do anything more than moan softly. She leaned forward, wrapping her hands around Mike's throat, and bucked faster.

From the amount of moisture building up on his stomach, Mike knew he was in the right place. Lolli bounced up and down on his dick feverishly, massaging his neck with her dainty fingers. As her grip tightened he knew she was close, so he thrust his hips harder. At some point he noticed that Lolli's fingers were tightening around his throat. She was squeezing so hard that it was becoming difficult to breathe. He tried to pry her hands loose, but Lolli's grip was like steel. "Ease up," he rasped.

"Shut up, I'm almost there." She kept riding and choking him.

Mike felt the lights in the room go dim. The look on Lolli's face was disturbing. Her lips were drawn into a sneer, and he could've sworn he saw her hazel eyes flash blue. Lolli was cutting off the flow of blood to his face and it seemed to all be diverted to his dick, making it swell. Mike was sure she would kill him if he didn't do something, so he started choking her back, which only seemed to turn her on.

"That's right, baby. Choke me like the little dog bitch that I am!" Lolli urged. With Mike's hands still secured around her neck, she arched her back and began throwing her hips in a circular motion. "Cum with me, Mike . . . cum with me!"

Spots danced before Mike's eyes from a lack of oxygen, but somehow he found the strength to keep pumping. "You fucking bitch!" he croaked as he exploded inside Lolli's hot box. He came so hard that he felt a tinge of pain when the hole in his dick stretched to accommodate the huge load passing through it.

Lolli kept stirring her hips, making sure she squeezed every ounce of cum out of Mike's dick. She remained perched, gently rocking back and forth, until she finally felt him start to go limp. "Touchdown," she whispered before dismounting him.

"You are one crazy fucking broad, Lollipop!" Mike gasped when he was finally free of her.

"Tell me something I don't know."

Lolli lay back on the pillow and retrieved a half-smoked joint from the ashtray.

"You could've killed me, you know," Mike said.

Lolli lit the joint and took a pull before responding. "Mike, if I wanted to kill you, strangulation wouldn't be my method of choice." She blew out a smoke ring. "I know sometimes I play a little rough, but you should be used to that by now."

"Nothing wrong with kinky sex, but you can save that sadistic shit for your white friends. I ain't with it."

Lolli rolled her eyes. "You got your nut off, didn't you? So stop acting like a little bitch. Now move your big-ass head, you're blocking the TV." She craned her neck to watch ESPN, which was airing football highlights from the night before.

Mike looked from the TV back to Lolli and shook his head. "I swear, sometimes I don't know who's the nigga and who's the bitch in this relationship." Every time he slept with Lolli, he was left feeling like a girl who had just given herself to a guy who she didn't realize was an asshole.

"I'm definitely *that* bitch," Lolli said, "but this ain't no relationship, so stop getting ahead of yourself."

"We've been fucking for over a year. If this isn't a relationship, what would you call it?"

"An arrangement." Lolli offered him the joint.

Mike waved his hand and muttered, "I'm good." He hopped out of bed and began pulling on his clothes. Lolli watched as he buttoned his jeans.

"What, you in your feelings now?"

Mike ignored her.

Lolli slid off the bed and eased herself behind Mike. She draped her arms around his neck, gently dragging her blue-painted fingernails down his chest and abs. "Stop acting like that, Mike," she whispered into his ear. "You know I love you."

Mike shrugged her off of him. "You don't love me, Lolli. You love fucking with my head. Every time we hook up it's the same shit. We party like a couple, fuck like a couple, and when things seem like they're finally falling together for us, you push me away and then I don't hear from you again until the next time you need your itch scratched. I'm sick of it!"

"If you're so sick of it, why do you always come whenever I call?" Lolli responded.

Mike was at a temporary loss for words. In all honesty, he had no idea why he came running whenever Lolli called. Lately, he had promised himself that he wouldn't give in, but then her name popped up on his phone and next thing you know, he was going to see her. He turned to her and said, "Because I'm a fucking idiot."

"You're not an idiot, Mike. You're just a man who follows his heart. Look, I know I can be a bitch sometimes, but I'm dealing with a lot. You know better than anybody else who I am and what I come from, so you should understand why I have to put my obligations to my family above my heart. In our line of work, being in love can get you killed."

"Bullshit. You're twenty-three, graduated at the top of your class at Spelman, own a nail salon, and are the heiress to a multimillion-dollar empire. You haven't been a soldier in your father's army for years, so save that conflicted-soul shit for somebody who doesn't know you, *Lauren.*"

Lolli folded her arms across her chest and frowned. "Yes, I'm fortunate to have some legitimate holdings that keep me comfortable, but that doesn't free me from my obligations to the other side of the family business. My daddy is the king of Five Points, but it takes a collective effort from all of us for him to hold that position. I can't speak for the next bitch, but I am bound by duty, honor, and loyalty to serve my family in any and all capacities required of me. I will always put my family first, and if you can't accept that, then I don't know what to tell you."

"Nobody is asking you *not* to put your family first. All I'm saying is why can't there be a balance between love and duty? Ghost has a fiancée and a kid and I don't see it affecting how he handles his business. As a matter of fact, he's actually more pleasant to be around since his daughter was born. It calmed his crazy ass down."

"I'm not my brother," Lolli shot back. "What Ghost does works for Ghost and what Lolli does works for Lolli. I understand what you're saying, Mike, but I'm on a paper chase and honestly don't have time for relationships. I hope you don't think I'm being cruel."

"No, you're just being Lolli." Mike grabbed his jacket and headed for the door. He hesitated, hoping Lolli would at least try and stop him, but she didn't. "Tell your mom happy birthday for me."

"You can tell her yourself at the party tonight."

"It's probably for the best that I put a little space between us for a minute."

"What? I hurt your little feelings and now you're not coming?" Lolli wanted Mike to be there, but wouldn't say so out loud. Her bleeding heart wasn't for display. Not for Mike, not for anyone. "You've been on me for some months now to plug you in with my brother," she said. "Tonight was supposed to be that night." It was sort of true. Mike had long been asking her to connect him with Ghost. Generally, Lolli didn't involve herself in management decisions within the family, but Mike was a different case. He was solid, inside and out. A young dude who had the potential to be heavy if only given the chance. Mike had a beautiful dick, but an even more beautiful mind. Bringing Mike into the family would keep her crush close and it would go on her résumé, another asset delivered to the family. Lolli had been stringing him along for a minute. Maybe it was time to finally close the deal.

Mike was silent as he weighed what Lolli had said about introducing him to Ghost. He opened his mouth as if he wanted to say something, then paused as if he'd thought better of it. Finally he said, "You still don't get it, do you? I'm over holding onto hope that one day you'll do right be me. Shit, you can't even do right by yourself." He let out a sad chuckle. "Take care of yourself, Lauren."

Mike made his exit, slamming the door behind him. On the way out, he passed Lolli's bodyguard, Nefertiti, in the hallway. She sat on a stool with her face buried in a book as if she hadn't been eavesdropping. She glanced up from her novel and gave Mike a knowing smirk, which only rubbed salt in his fresh wound. Mike and Nefertiti did not get along. She felt like he was a bad influence on Lolli and Mike felt the same way about her. Mike wanted to slap the smirk off her face, but the last thing he needed at that moment was to get into a fistfight with her. Not only because she was a female, but because she was also a Reaper.

When a soft knock tapped on the door, Lolli lay ass-naked in the bed, her feet crossed at the ankles, finishing her joint. She ignored it, continuing her weed session and channel surfing. She knew who it was and what they wanted. After a few seconds of unanswered knocking, Lolli heard the swipe of a key card and the sound of the door lock releasing. Some people were so predictable.

Nefertiti opened the door just wide enough to slide her sleek frame through. She learned a long time ago not to fully open any door that Lauren "Lollipop" King was behind. There was no telling what you would see, and it wouldn't do for a random passerby to get an eyeful of her shenanigans. Nefertiti had made the mistake only once, when they were at the MGM Grand in Vegas. The end result found Lolli's name headlined across several blogs. The reporter had been disguised as a member of the hotel cleaning crew, which was how he'd managed to secure the lucky snapshot of her in the room. When Chancellor King found out, the scandal almost cost Nefertiti her job. The only thing that saved her was that it wasn't really her fault. She had heard screaming coming from inside the room and reacted as she was supposed to by rushing to protect Lolli. Never in a million years would she have thought that when she swung that door open she'd find the heiress in the middle of a three-way with a couple she'd met at the casino. Ever since then, Nefertiti never opened Lolli's door wider than she needed to.

She closed the door now and went to stand at the foot of Lolli's bed. Her posture was military straight, but her eyes were loose and fluid, taking in everything in the room, including her boss. Nefertiti wore her usual black pantsuit with a black shirt beneath. The outfit made her look like a member of the Secret Service. Nefertiti was fond of wearing black because of how the color swallowed her charcoal skin. In the right light, she could blend seamlessly with the shadows. Her jacket fit snugly enough to show off her small waistline, but maintained enough room to conceal her ever-present .45 in its shoulder holster.

"I don't recall telling you to come in," Lolli said, not looking away from the television.

"Your friend left in a bit of a rush, so I was just making sure you were okay," Nefertiti explained.

Lolli looked at her then. "You've been seeing Mike climb in and out of my bed for a while now. I'm sure you realize that he isn't a threat."

"Mike might be your part-time lover, but he's also a known killer. Men like him are always a threat, even if they don't mean to be."

"What if I told you I was thinking about making him more than part-time?"

"May I speak freely?"

Lolli shrugged. "Since when have you needed permission to add your two cents?"

"Mike is a good guy but he ain't for you," Nefertiti said.

Lolli raised an eyebrow. "And what makes you say that?"

"He's a street nigga."

"I'm a King—we're all from the dirt, Nefertiti."

"No, *we* aren't. I'm from the dirt, Mike is from the dirt, even Ghost has had his taste of hard times. But not you. By the time the princess was born, Chance had already begun his ascension."

"Are you saying I haven't put in any work for this family?"

"Not at all, Lolli. We all know your skills at espionage as unparalleled, and you play a large role in your father's . . . *affairs*. But there's a difference. Your life was already mapped out by the time you came into this world. The rest of us had to fight and figure it out along the way."

"Fuck you, Nefertiti!" Lolli jumped out of bed and approached her bodyguard, standing toe to toe with her. "I'll kick your ass and ten bitches that look just like you if they get in my way."

Nefertiti smirked. "Lolli, remember what your therapist said about that temper."

Lolli balled her fists up. "You think I'm joking?"

"Come on, Lolli. Let's not do this today."

"What, you scared now? Not the last of the big bad Reapers scared of little old me." Lolli shoved her.

Nefertiti sighed. "This ain't Burger King but have it your way. Same stakes?"

"You know it," Lolli said, taking a defensive stance.

Nefertiti slipped out of her suit jacket. She had barely gotten it over her arms when Lolli sucker-punched her.

Lolli had Nefertiti at a disadvantage so she tried to press her attack. But Nefertiti was swift and wrapped her suit jacket around Lolli's arms, tying her in it like a strait jacket. She was now behind Lolli holding her tight in the fabric.

"Do you yield?" Nefertiti whispered into her ear.

"A King never yields!"

Lolli braced her feet against the hotel room's dresser and pushed backward, sending her and Nefertiti crashing to the floor. The two women rolled around, trading blows and counterstrikes. Nefertiti was pleasantly surprised when Lolli managed to land a few punches to her exposed ribs and gut. She had been practicing. Lolli was good, but Nefertiti had the experience. She managed to roll Lolli onto her back and press her forearm against her throat, cutting off her air.

"Yield?" she said.

Lolli struggled, but it was useless. Had it been a real fight, Nefertiti could've easily ended her. "Okay," she wheezed, "you got it."

Nefertiti removed her forearm from Lolli's throat and balanced herself above her defeated opponent. "Now pay up."

"Sometimes I fucking hate you," Lolli sighed before grabbing Nefertiti by the back of her head and pulling her in for a kiss.

CHAPTER 4

I t was just after eight a.m. when the black town car carrying Chancellor King pulled to a stop in front of Morning Star Meats. It was a drab little butcher shop and café in Williamsburg where you could procure all you kosher meat needs and enjoy a bitter cup of coffee. It wasn't much to look at, but people in the neighborhood swore by it for their cuts. Besides being a community landmark, Morning Star also served as a place where important men could meet to have serious conversations.

Little Stevie was the first to step out of the car. He shook the folds of his black overcoat to dislodge any lint, stomping his high-polished black Stacy Adams on the concrete. Although he could be considered small—standing a shade over five five—that wasn't how he had earned his moniker. He had been dubbed Little Stevie after the famous singer because he always wore black sunglasses and sported cornrows with colorful beads at the ends. He'd rocked this hairstyle since the seventies, and even as age crept in and his hairline had receded, he still refused to cut his hair. When it became too short on the top, he took to wearing hats.

Stevie was in his fifties but carried himself like a much younger man. He worked out regularly, drank plenty of water, and minded his own business. If you asked him why he was such a zealot about his body he'd always say the same thing: "I stay ready just in case I ever have the misfortune of bumping into a young nigga who done got liquored up and decided he wants to show his ass for his birthday." If you understood it, this was a stone-cold Little Stevie jewel. He was good with his fists but gifted with pistols. His hands were Old West fast; he'd shot more than a dozen men since he'd been in the service of Chancellor King.

After surveying the block to ensure everything was clear, Stevie motioned to the two passengers in the back.

Delores Reese, who was affectionately called Chippie, exited the vehicle next. She was a tall brown drink of water, with full lips and thick black hair pulled into a tight bun. Cinnamon eyes hid behind her thick black glasses, which seemed to slide down her nose every few minutes, forcing her to adjust them. When Chippie cleaned herself up she turned every man's head, but her everyday style was usually Plain Jane. She wasn't big on glam or dressing up. In fact, the only pieces in her closet that didn't make her look like a schoolteacher had been picked out by either Maureen or Lolli. She was a quiet woman and never said more than she needed to, but she watched everything. That was her job—to watch and interpret. She was the only woman outside of the family who could put her mouth in his business.

Last but certainly not least to step out of the town car was the king. When you first laid eyes on Chancellor King, he looked nothing like what you'd expect based on the stories of his exploits and the weight of his name. He was of modest height, around five nine. Well into his fifties, his wavy black hair was still thick and full, but strands of gray had begun to show in his dark beard. Per usual, he wore an all-black outfit, his ruby-encrusted wedding band the only splash of color.

Chippie stood in front of Chance but behind Stevie. She glared at the establishment with distaste; it was a slum and somewhere she'd rather not be. On the other side of the window she could see a man sitting on a stool watching them. His head was cocked, listening to someone beyond Chippie's line of vision. He nodded and stood, walking to the door to meet them.

"I don't like this," Chippie said.

The man wore a cotton jogging suit and track sneakers. One side of his jacket dipped a bit, suggesting he was carrying something with weight to it. His whole persona screamed organized crime.

"How many times do I have to tell you that we're good?" Stevie said. "I know the guy who runs this joint. He and I go back a taste. Besides, this place is sacred ground. Ain't nobody gonna try shit. Even if they did, I'd make 'em regret it."

Chippie looked to Chance, who just shrugged. "If Stevie says we're good," he said, "then I'm inclined to believe him."

The man in the jogging suit held the door open for the trio. He waited until they crossed the threshold before informing them that he needed to pat them down.

"Let me save you the trouble," Little Stevie said, unbuttoning his coat. There was a large handgun hanging from a leather shoulder holster. "I'm packing and I ain't got no plans for giving it up."

The man in the jogging suit looked like he was about to give them a problem when a voice announced, "It's okay, Phillip. He's good."

Phillip moved aside so that they could pass.

Stevie led the trio inside, where they encountered the man who the voice belonged to. He stood behind the butcher's counter wearing a blood-soiled smock, wiping down the edge of a very large cleaver with a rag. He appeared to be in his early sixties, with thinning black hair flaked with gray and a bushy handlebar mustache. His deeply tanned skin and aquiline features suggested that he had been born somewhere other than on US soil—somewhere in the Middle East, maybe. Cold brown eyes sat behind wire-framed glasses, which remained glued to the trio as they crossed the room. When they reached the counter, he slammed his knife into a nearby butcher's block and glared at the group. "If you people are looking for the fried chicken joint, it's a few blocks over," he said in heavily accented English.

"Nah, I was kind of in the mood for *turkey* today," Stevie said, making a pun on the man's nationality—Turkish. Never taking his eyes off the butcher, Stevie pushed his jacket open to show the gun.

The butcher removed a curved gutting knife from the sink and darted around the counter. He stood a few feet away from Stevie, twirling the knife between his fingers.

"That might prove to be a bit too tough for those dentures of yours," Stevie snarled.

Chippie took a step back, but Chance remained where he was. A moment of thick tension hung in the room. Just when it seemed like it was about to pop off, Little Stevie flashed a smile.

"Good ol' Ahmad. Forever the ball-breaker!"

The two embraced without dropping their weapons.

"My favorite spade!" Ahmad said affectionately, patting Stevie on the back. "When was the last time I saw you? Ten years ago?"

"Fifteen," Stevie said.

"Is everything okay?" a young man asked from somewhere in the back. He too was dressed in a butcher's smock and held a knife. Despite his skin being slightly darker than Ahmad's and his hair slightly coarser, the resemblance between the two men was obvious.

"Everything is fine," Ahmad assured him. "My youngest, Terrence," he told Stevie.

"Turk," the youngster said, preferring to be called by his street name.

"We're good here, Terrence," Ahmad said. "Why don't you go finish carving up the brisket for me. I promised Mrs. Schulman we'd have it done by noon." He flicked his knife across the room to his son, who caught it by the handle. Ahmad waited until Turk was behind the butcher's counter before turning his attention back to Stevie. "Sorry, you know how kids can be."

"I wasn't fool enough to have any," Stevie replied. "In all the time we've known each other, I never heard you talk of having a son, only daughters."

"Terrence and I are only recently acquainted," Ahmad said in a way that told Stevie he didn't want to get into it right now.

"You bringing him into the business?" Stevie asked.

"Terrence was already in the business when he came to me. I'm just showing him how to play the game well enough to where he doesn't get killed. The Turk, as they call him, is quite gifted with a blade, but still rough around the edges when it comes to tact."

"If he's anything like his old man, I don't think that will be an issue," Stevie said, recalling some of the tales attached to Ahmad's name. "And your daughters: how are they?"

"Allison is away at school, studying law, of all things," Ahmad said with a chuckle. "Beula lives out west with her husband and my two grandsons."

"Wow, you're a granddad? Congratulations."

"Thanks to you. Had you not done what you did for my baby, I'd have been paying for her funeral instead of her wedding. I'll never forget you stepping in for my Beula when she got tangled up with those colored hoods in Flatbush."

Beula was a wild child. Several years earlier, she had gotten herself mixed up with some Haitian drug dealers and hooked on heroin, running the streets acting crazy—robbing, lying, whoring, and doing whatever it took to get a fix. One day, she and her boyfriend at the time thought it wise to rob one of the dealers they hustled for. The end result left Beula's boyfriend dead and her running for her life. It would only have been a matter of time before the Haitians caught up with her and buried her in a hole next to her boyfriend. Luckily, she was saved by a miracle. As it turned out, Little Stevie had business dealings with the Haitians. When he found out about Beula's troubles, he stepped in on the girl's behalf and brokered a deal for her life.

"What are friends for?" Stevie said now.

"Speaking of friends," Ahmad said, looking over at Chance.

"Damn, where are my manners? Ahmad, this is one of my oldest and dearest friends, Chance King."

Ahmad gave a respectful nod. "The man who launched the rainbow coalition."

"So they say," Chance replied modestly.

"And Chance, this is a friend of ours, Ahmad Kaplan," Stevie said, patting Ahmad on the back.

"Who in the underworld doesn't know the Butcher of the Kore District?" Chance said. The Butcher had been a legend long before arriving in the US in the late seventies. He had cut and killed his way out of the district and built a career for himself doing contract hits in the States. The Butcher was hired to do *nasty* jobs—he had a flare for violence. Chance approached him and they shook hands. "The last I heard, you had retired."

"I have," Ahmad said with a shrug. "I'm only here as a go-between as a favor to Stevie. Other than that, I'm out of the game."

"Bullshit!" Stevie butted in. "I'll bet that if the bag was right you wouldn't have a problem sharpening up that hatchet of yours and splitting some poor bastard from the rooter to the tooter!"

"Let's hope for both of our sakes that that's a wager you'll never have to make," Ahmad said. "Now, onto the business."

"I appreciate you allowing us to have this meeting here," Chance said.

Ahmad nodded. "Mr. Schulman is waiting for you in the back. Unfortunately, because of the sensitive nature of your business, he's requested that whatever is said stays between the two of you. Your people will have to wait."

"No problem," Stevie said. "You go on and handle your business, Chance. Me and Ahmad can keep Chippie occupied by telling her some of our old war stories."

"I can even fix you guys some sandwiches while you wait. We've got the freshest meat in the city," Ahmad boasted.

"Thanks but no thanks, old friend," said Stevie. "I know how you made some of those bodies disappear back in the day, and respectfully, we won't be eating anything out of this joint."

Chance ventured behind the counter and through a door that led to a back room with several small tables. At one of these tables sat Paul Schulman, sipping an espresso with his back to the wall and a manicured pinkie finger extended. Paul looked like an old movie star, with loose tresses and frigid blue eyes. His tailored gray suit coat stopped just shy of his wrist and the collar of his white shirt had been starched within an inch of its life. The top three buttons were undone, and a V of exposed skin showed a silver pendant bearing the Star of David.

Chance and Paul weren't friends but they were cordial. Their paths often crossed in business dealings. Paul was a member of a small group of Jewish businessmen led by Paul's uncle, Benjamin Levitz. Paul's family owned several jewelry stores throughout the city and serviced everyone from the rich and famous to the criminally inclined. They didn't discriminate when it came to profit. Through his jewelry business, among other things, Benjamin had made some very powerful contacts over the years.

Unlike Benjamin, who was more of a businessman, Paul was a gangster. Behind the tailored suits and charming smile lurked a man who had been through *some things*. He'd gotten his first taste of the criminal lifestyle as a lad running around the streets of Queens with a crew of neighborhood kids who called themselves the Flushing Boys. Although they established a reputation of being tough guys and petty thieves, Paul aimed for bigger scores. He had been raised in the jewelry business so he knew the quality of stones better than most and had the outlets to fence them. When Benjamin caught wind of it, he wasn't pleased, but he didn't refuse the merchandise his nephew brought him. Benjamin turned a blind eye to Paul's shenanigans so long as there was no heat on him and he got his taste off the top. Thanks to Paul, his uncle's jewelry business was booming. Chance knew all of this, of course, but he hadn't come to talk about ice.

Paul eyed Chance over the rim of his espresso cup. He let the older Black man stand for a few ticks before inviting him to take the empty seat across from him—an intentional slight. This was Paul's way of telling Chance that they were on his home turf and that Paul would be the one who dictated the conversation. He let the silence linger between them before finally saying, "Welcome, King of Five Points."

"That king bullshit is used by grunts and people who address me by my last name. I've always just been Chance amongst my friends."

"Is that what we are now? Friends?" Paul set his espresso cup down. "I can count on one hand how many times you've ever bothered to speak to me if it didn't involve business with my uncle or the High Court."

"Blame it on my head and not my heart," Chance said. "We'll be thick as thieves when you hear why I asked to meet."

"It must be important for you to request such a discrete rendezvous. I mean, I'm all for discretion, but this could give some of our mutual associates the wrong idea," Paul said, referencing the governing body of Five Points, the High Court. "Maybe I should've let my uncle in on this?"

"You're still welcome to do so, if you like. Though I think by the time I'm done you'll understand what you stand to gain by keeping your mouth shut."

"You think that imaginary crown on your head holds more weight than my loyalty to my uncle?"

"Not at all, but your loyalty to your own best interests will ensure your silence. I'm here to offer you something that you could probably use right about now."

"And what's that?" Paul asked.

"A lifeline."

Paul cocked his head slightly to the left. "Now why would I need a lifeline?"

"To keep you from drowning—why else?"

"I assure you, my ship is airtight."

"There are some who would beg to differ," Chance countered. "Rumor has it that things have been a little tense between the two of you lately."

Paul gave a shrug. "That's not a rumor, it's a fact. My uncle has never approved of my extracurricular activities, but we make our arrangement work."

Though he downplayed it, the rift between Paul and his

uncle had been growing steadily for some time. Paul wanted to take the organization into the new millennium, but Benjamin kept him on a short leash. It had caused some tension in the organization between the youths and the elders. It was a family issue; few outside the circle were aware of such tribulations. Yet here was Chancellor King, waving the information before Paul like a loaded gun.

"Right," Chance continued. "He turns a blind eye to your exploits so long as your shit doesn't spill onto his clean floors. You've been doing a hell of a job at keeping your two worlds from colliding, until now."

"You gonna keep talking in riddles or spit out whatever it is you've come here to say? You're not the only person on my calendar today."

Chance folded his hands on the table and stared directly into Paul's eyes. "I hear your uncle's greatest fears are about to come to fruition. The prince of Hebrews is about to burn and take the whole kingdom with him."

Paul leaned forward. When he spoke, his movie-star face disappeared—in its place came the leader of the Flushing Boys. "Be careful, Your Highness. This isn't Five Points. You can't sling threats in here without repercussions. We make you stand on your words at this end of town."

"I'm afraid you've misunderstood me, Paul. I didn't come here to threaten you. No, I came to enlighten you. The feds are trying to build a case against you."

"So what? They've been the bump on my ass for years and still haven't managed to tie me to anything thus far."

"But now they have an informant. Someone who can tie you directly to a federal crime."

Paul breathed a sigh of relief. It had been almost a year since he'd gotten his hands truly dirty, and since then he had always given orders through a third party. He made it a point to keep himself insulated and therefore it was near impossible to directly link him to any of his numerous crimes. There was no way Chance's information could be accurate.

"Listen," Paul said, "I'm afraid you've been misinformed and, as a result, wasted both our time. Now, if you'll excuse me." He rose from the table as if to dismiss Chance, but the king wasn't done.

"Ira Sherman," Chance said.

"What about him?" Ira was a member of Paul's crew and one of the few people he dealt with regularly.

"Went missing a few weeks back, didn't he?"

"I wouldn't call it missing. He took some time to fly out west to visit his sick mother," Paul said.

"Can anybody verify that?" Chance asked. "You see a plane ticket? Has he called to check in with you?"

Paul hadn't heard from Ira in the week or so that he'd been gone. He had reasoned that Ira was just busy with his mother, but truthfully he hadn't put much thought into the situation.

"Of course he didn't," Chance said without waiting for Paul's response. "Ira's not in California. He's right downtown in a federal holding cell while they hammer out the details of his agreement. While you've been trying to keep your nose clean for the sake of your organization, some of your boys have been doing rogue shit on the side. Ira's been knocking off cigarette trucks and reselling the product to stores in the ghetto. Unfortunately, he got himself caught in a sting. With him already having a record, they were going to hit him with at least a dime. But ol' Ira decided he wasn't built to do hard time, so he threw them a bigger fish—you!"

"If you come in here trying to brand a member of my crew as a rat, you'd better have more than words to validate the accusation!" Paul barked. He struggled to keep his anger in check. He couldn't let Chance have the upper hand.

"I figured you'd feel that way," Chance said, reaching into the front pocket of his suit jacket to remove his phone. He thumbed a few keys and, seconds later, Paul's cell pinged.

Paul picked up his phone and opened the file Chance had sent him. It was a closed-circuit video that showed a small room. There was no sound, but the picture was clear. A man in a white shirt with his sleeves rolled to the elbow stood in the corner watching two men sitting around a small table. One was dressed in a cheap suit that screamed law enforcement, and the second was none other than Ira.

Even without being able to hear what was being said, Paul could guess what was going on. "Where did you get this?"

"You're asking the wrong question, Paul," Chance said with a smug edge. "Where I got it isn't as important as what you plan to do about it. Word gets out that you've let a weasel into your uncle's hen house, they'll nail your pretty ass to a cross faster than they did Jesus."

"You come in here trying to shake me down, old man?"

"Friends don't shake friends down. They offer them solutions."

"Chance, we're both from the streets. We know there's only one solution to a rodent problem," Paul said.

"Not when you've got friends with reach," Chance said. "Killing Ira isn't out of the question, but it's not the wisest course of action. What's done is done with him, and the feds are going to get their scapegoat, but this doesn't mean it has to be the one he promised them."

"If not me, then who?"

"You let me worry about that. All you need to know is that I'm going to make it so Ira points his finger elsewhere and the government will accept the offering."

"And what's this going to cost me?" Paul wanted to know.

Chance smiled wide and leaned across the table. "Only to leave here knowing I made a real friend. Are we friends, Paul?" He extended his hand.

Paul stared at the hand as if it were a poisonous snake. No matter how many different scenarios he wheeled around in his head, they all came back to Chance having him by the balls. He stood and took the man's hand in his. "Yes, Mr. King, I believe we are."

As their palms met, something eerie passed between them. This was a devil's bargain to be sure, but owing Chancellor King beat the alternative.

"Actually," Chance said, as if an afterthought, "there is one small thing I'll be needing of you in return for making this go away, *friend*."

CHAPTER 5

S hadow and his family were finishing up breakfast when a soft tap sounded at the back door. Shadow assumed a family associate was stopping by; all other callers came by way of the front door. Ghost moved to stand, but Shadow jumped up and said, "I got it!"

He rushed to the door, eager to greet their guest. The men employed by his father and brother were dangerous, but they were also a colorful lot. Shadow did his best to hang around them when their paths crossed in the streets because he was thirsty to soak up the game they kicked. He especially looked forward to the times when they came to the house because that usually meant something big was brewing.

Standing on the steps outside the back door was his cousin Monster. His government name was Melvin; Monster was a moniker given to him by his mother. "You're a cruel little bastard—a monster," she used to tell him. Monster was the kind of kid who used to set kittens on fire for kicks. He was as ugly on the inside as he was on the outside. His face was one that only a mother could love, and even she could barely stand to look at him. He had dark eyes that were slightly off-center, a flat nose, and big lips that had darkened over the years from smoking so many blunts. His most disturbing feature, though, was his large, misshapen head, which awkwardly balanced on his vein-streaked neck. Scars marked his worn face, courtesy of his many battles on the streets as well as in the prison system—

the most pronounced of them being a slash that went from his left cheek up across his head and stopped at the base of his neck. He'd lost half his ear on the day he received that scar, but the man who cut him lost his life.

"'Sup, lil' nigga," Monster said in his gravelly voice, palming Shadow's head.

"Watch my waves," Shadow complained, moving away from Monster's mammoth mitt. He brought his hand over his dark hair to smooth it back out. Monster stepped inside the house, but Shadow stopped him. "I know you got something for me, Cuzzo."

Monster flashed a crooked grin. "Don't I always?" His plotting eyes peeked into the kitchen to make sure no one could see what he was doing, then he dipped his hand into his pocket. After fishing around for a second, he produced a pair of brass knuckles. Shadow turned the brutish weapon over in his hands and frowned.

"Cuz, I thought you was finally about to lay a pole on me and you bust out with some *Fight Club* shit? What the hell am I supposed to do with this?"

"Get a nigga off your ass in a tight situation," Monster replied, before taking the brass knuckles from Shadow. He slipped them over his own thick fingers and flexed them. "See, you young niggas are soft. Shit jumps off and the first thing your brains tell you to do is grab a pistol. What happens when you can't get to that rod and gotta knuckle up? Let's say two or three jokers get the drop and you find yourself ass-naked with no iron. Your only hope of survival is a good old-fashioned brawl. One taste of these is all you need to tip the odds in your favor." Monster punched the brass knuckles into the palm of his other hand. "You bust one nigga's head open and it'll give the rest of them food for thought. Trust me on that." He handed the brass knuckles back to Shadow.

"I'd still rather have a gun," Shadow mumbled before slipping the brass knuckles into his pocket.

"What are you two devils over there conspiring about?" Maureen asked from the kitchen.

Monster lumbered in with Shadow trailing behind him. "How you this morning, Auntie?" Monster leaned in to give Maureen a kiss on the cheek. "I'm just giving Shadow here a hard time."

"Busy as ever. And isn't it a bit early to be hitting the sauce?" Maureen asked, smelling the liquor on his breath.

"Time passes differently when you don't sleep," Monster answered.

"I hope your ass is sober enough to drive," Ghost said, pushing himself up from the table and sliding on his jacket. "We've got a lot of ground to cover."

"I been chauffeuring your ass around for the better part of a year and ain't got you in a wreck yet, have I?" Monster sneered. Just then he noticed Chapman eyeballing him. "'Sup, Unc?"

"Monster," Chapman said, as if the name tasted like ashes in his mouth, "you off to strangle kittens this morning?"

"Not yet, but killing a pussy is definitely on my to-do list."

"*Monster,*" Maureen said sternly.

"Sorry, Auntie," he said without looking away from Chapman.

"You hungry, nephew?" Maureen asked him.

Before Monster could respond, Ghost answered for him: "Nah, we got moves to make. See y'all later on."

Ghost kissed his mother and moved toward the back door.

"Y'all be safe out there and please be on time for the party tonight," Maureen said. "Are you and your girlfriend coming too, Monster?"

Embarrassment flashed across Monster's face. "Oh, uh—I didn't know anything about a party."

"I'll fill him in, Mama," Ghost said over his shoulder.

Monster followed, but not before flashing a murderous look at Chapman.

"What is it with you two?" Maureen asked Chapman after Ghost and Monster had left.

"Whatever do you mean?" Chapman said between two big gulps of coffee.

"You two are family but you couldn't tell from the way you act toward each other. That's your brother's only son."

"Monster might have Colt's blood, but not his character. He's a devil. Being in the same room with him gives me the creeps."

"There are some who say the same about you," Maureen said. "You ain't hardly no saint, Chapman."

"Of course not. I'm a King. We're all power-hungry killers, or haven't you heard?"

Chapman's phone vibrated on the table. For as quickly as he snatched it up, you'd have thought someone had just dropped their wallet. Shadow took note of the sneaky grin that appeared on his uncle's face when he slunk out of the kitchen to take the call.

"No, Chapman, I don't need any help cleaning up," Maureen called out after him. Her brother-in-law kept walking as if he didn't even hear her. "Lazy bastard," she muttered.

"I got it, Ma," Shadow said, collecting dishes from the table and scraping their contents into the trash. He always offered to help his mom without her having to ask—he was a good son that way. Besides, Shadow could read his mother's moods better than most, and he could tell that something was weighing on her. He wanted to help her carry it in any way that he could.

Despite her complaint, Maureen was glad to have Chapman out of her kitchen and her face. He worked her nerves, and it didn't help that his little slip of the lip had raised a question that Maureen wasn't quite sure she was ready to answer. In truth, she was just as skeptical about this business with her husband and the new direction he wanted to go in, but as his wife and consigliere she would never confess to this.

Maureen knew that Chancellor accepted the legacy his father left him more out of obligation than an actual desire to run a criminal enterprise. Although Chance had been more into school than the streets, when the time came for him to take his father's place, he did so without complaint. He was an adept hustler, but his morality was his Achilles' heel. Every illegal move he made was tinged with guilt, a nagging uncertainty that he was doing the *wrong* thing. And while he was a natural when it came to playing the streets, his heart wasn't into it. This was why Maureen indulged his political ambitions. At first, politics seemed like a harmless distraction from Chance's real work, a place where he could wash his hands when he was done playing in the mud. No one expected him to actually be a *good* politician, especially not Maureen. It was her own fault for underestimating her husband. Chance excelled at whatever he did and this was no different. He was a gifted politician, highly skilled at schmoozing and dealmaking. Of course this worried Maureen. Between Second Chance Realty and the income Chance drew from being a city official, the Kings had enough money to live on for years. But this wasn't about money. It was about the power that came with being queen. It was something she wasn't ready to give up yet.

"Did you hear me, Ma?" Shadow asked, snapping his mother out of her daze.

"Huh?"

He held up a printout from the kitchen counter. "What is this?"

"Just a copy of the seating chart for tonight."

"Then somebody must've made a mistake, because they've placed this Zaza family at our table," Shadow said, frowning at the piece of paper. The name Zaza was familiar to him, but he couldn't place it. He did know that a Zaza wasn't a King. And Kings sat with Kings.

"No, baby," Maureen said, "it's not a mistake. Orlando Zaza is an old friend of the family. He and your daddy used to be in business together until they had a difference of opinion. They've recently decided to reconcile. Seeing the Zazas and Kings break bread will send a very strong message to those watching."

"Boss move," Shadow said with a smile.

"Orlando will be bringing his family with him," Maureen continued. "His wife and youngest daughter. Josette's about your age and has her daddy wrapped around her finger the same as you do with Chance. That being said, I'm going to need you to do your part to make sure that she enjoys herself tonight."

"You do know that I can take that the wrong way, right?" Shadow said, playfully raising his eyebrows.

"You keep that hot cock of yours under control tonight, Sean. I don't want the girl deflowered, at least not yet. For tonight? Just make sure that Josette's comfortable. That she feels like she's amongst family. You think you can do that?"

"I got you, Ma."

"That's my boy." Maureen kissed him on both cheeks. "Now, don't you have somewhere to be?"

"About to take off. You need anything before I go?"

"No, baby. And thank you again for holding your mama down. I know sometimes we're tasked to do things that we might not like or agree with, but we put our personal feelings aside for the good of the family."

"Absolutely, Ma. All for the family." It was a mantra Shadow had known since he was a tot. "I'm about to call an Uber and start making moves."

"No, your daddy clocks that Uber account and I don't want him to know where you're going." Maureen walked to the board on the wall where several sets of car keys hung. She inspected two sets before settling on the keys to her Mercedes.

Surprised, Shadow caught the keys his mother threw him. She never let anyone drive her car. "You must want to see Millie bad if you're letting me take your whip."

"It's important that we show a unified front tonight. I need all Kings on deck. Just make sure you're careful out there."

"I'm gonna link up with Fresh and Pain. They'll hold me down." Shadow started for the door but paused as he reached the threshold. "What if I can't find her?"

"You will. Of all my children, you're the only one who never disappoints."

CHAPTER 6

Forty minutes after her second romp, Lolli was showered, dressed, and riding in the back of her black Navigator across the George Washington Bridge into New Jersey. She wasn't in a rush so the traffic didn't bother her. Besides, the person she was visiting had no idea she was coming. As she lounged across the leather seats, she deftly twisted a blunt of some shit she had forgotten the name of. Whatever it was, it smelled like flowers. She lit it and inhaled, holding the smoke in her lungs for a time before exhaling.

When she looked up at the rearview mirror, she noticed Nefertiti watching her. When their eyes met, Nefertiti looked sharply away. Lolli ignored her. Nefertiti didn't like when Lolli smoked in the car, especially when they were riding dirty. The bodyguard had a concealed carry permit so they couldn't get into any real trouble, but who wanted the headache of getting stopped and searched? Still, Lolli needed to get blazed. She had a lot on her mind and it was necessary to sort some things out before reaching their destination.

Lolli was about to pull a bold and possibly ill-advised move, depending on who you asked. But she didn't have a choice. Things were unfolding faster than any of them had expected within the family and she needed to do her part to make sure they were covered. Lolli had an uncanny knack for identifying potential threats and neutralizing them before they manifested. Her father affectionately called her his "edge."

By the time Lolli tossed what was left of the blunt out the window, they were rolling through Ridgefield Park. It was more of a village than an actual city. Driving through the town center, Lolli took in the shops and an old-style movie theater. The layout reminded her of the backdrop of a Stephen King novel. Nefertiti steered them through the town with the familiarity of someone who had been there before. (Which she had. As a rule of thumb, Lolli's shadow always scouted their destinations when venturing into what could be considered enemy territory. This wasn't to say that the person they were meeting was an enemy, but she hadn't yet determined them to be a friend.)

Most of the driveways were still covered in snow from the blizzard that had dumped on the tristate a few days prior. In one of the yards, Lolli saw a family building a snowman. The husband and wife playfully tossed snow at each other before coating their children with sheets of powder. The kids ran in circles, giggling and brushing snow off their noses. Lolli was struck by a faint hint of sadness. She was a solitary soul who preferred her own company, but there were times when she became incredibly lonely. Despite her best intentions, she craved a home and family of her own. Yet there was no time for such stability. Her duty to her father's cause superseded her own needs.

Contrary to what most people thought, it wasn't easy being the only *biological* daughter of Chance King. Being the lone female in the house other than her mother meant she had to work twice as hard to prove that she was just as good at handling family business as her brothers. By tradition, the oldest male heir usually ascended to the head of the family—a sexist, stupid rule, if you asked Lolli. Her father was a great and just king, but what would happen when he was removed from the throne?

Chapman was Chance's older brother and the least qualified to lead, but the rule of succession had almost placed the crown on his head, which would've been a disaster. Had it not been for her grandfather, Edward, bending the rule to put Chance in power, Chapman would've surely run their family business into the ground. Now Ghost was next in line. Her big brother was solid and a good man at heart, but he was a better general than king. He excelled at war. Even when there weren't problems, he'd find a way to create one before long. The only other swinging dick on the King family tree was Shadow. Although she loved her baby brother, crowning him would've been nearly as poor a choice as crowning Chapman. Shadow had the looks, the charisma, and the pedigree, but he lacked the heart it took to do what would be asked of him as the next king. He was sheltered, immature, and selfish. A good king had to know how to put the needs of his subjects before his own. Shadow didn't fit the bill.

The only logical choice to succeed Chancellor, then, was Lolli. She had spent as much time studying under her father as Ghost had. She could play the boardroom just as well as a street corner. Lolli was skilled at closing both deals and caskets. The soldiers respected her. She deserved the crown, but in order to even be able to throw her hat in the ring, she would have to first show her father that she was a capable leader. This was exactly why she'd come to Ridgefield Park.

Nefertiti parked the Navigator along the sidewalk of a large redbrick house. Balloons decorated the front yard and doorway. The sounds of children playing in the backyard was audible even in the car. Nefertiti turned to Lolli in the backseat and said, "You sure this is a good idea?"

"Nope," Lolli answered, sliding out from the backseat and onto the front lawn. She paused to look at her reflection in the

SUV. She was dressed conservatively that day: a pink blouse, heels, and a black shirt that was tight enough to show off her curves without making her look like a slut. Not something she would normally be caught dead in, but she wanted to make a good first impression. With her hair pulled back into a pony-tail and wearing no makeup, Lolli could've easily passed for a schoolteacher—her desired effect. She wanted to appear as nonthreatening as possible.

She walked up the path and rang the doorbell. After a few seconds, she heard the lock clank. When the door flung open, Lolli was greeted by an older Black woman wearing a maid's uniform. "May I help you?" she asked.

"Yes, I'm here to see Alderman Porter," Lolli said in the most pleasant voice she could muster.

"Do you have an appointment?"

"No, but he'll see me. Tell him it's Lauren King."

The old woman gave her a leery look before disappearing inside the house. A few minutes later she returned wearing a sour expression. She opened the door wider and smiled falsely. "Right this way, Ms. King."

The maid led Lolli through an expansive living room that boasted a huge fireplace with beautiful paintings hanging on the wall above it. Upon close inspection, Lolli determined that the works were authentic. She had received a degree in art from Arizona State University, which usually proved to be as useful as a flaccid penis. Yet it had taught her how to tell the difference between a forgery and a real piece of art, a skill that occasionally served her well.

Lolli trotted behind the maid down a long hallway, sneaking glances through the windows into the backyard. About two dozen kids ran around the property playing games, while a pop star, whose name escaped Lolli, stood beside a photo booth taking pictures and signing autographs. Lolli had seen photos of Porter's primary residence on the Upper East Side, but this mini-mansion in New Jersey had come as a surprise; not too many city officials kept second homes in Jersey. Lolli was no financial wizard, but based on what she knew about what her father brought in working as a city official, the alderman seemed to be living well above his pay grade.

The maid escorted Lolli into a room at the end of the hall, which Lolli assumed was the alderman's office.

"Have a seat. Alderman Porter will be with you shortly."

After the maid disappeared, Lolli acquainted herself with the office. Framed photographs of Alderman Porter with other elected officials were displayed on the bookshelf, which dominated an entire wall. She moved to the desk, where she picked up a family portrait that sat next to his computer. In their matching sweaters and Colgate smiles, the Porters looked like the typical all-American family. When her eyes landed on the young man standing to the right of the alderman, she almost dropped the photo. She brought it up to eye level to get a better look. The boy's skin was light, with only the faintest hints of melanin, but he stood out against the rest of the family's pure white skin. His lack of resemblance to any of the other Porters suggested that he wasn't a biological child, yet there he stood among the older children like a proud son. Lolli had thought she knew everything there was to know about Alderman Porter— apparently, she'd been wrong. His home appeared to be rich with secrets.

"Ms. King," a voice called out from behind her. She quickly set the photo back on the desk and twisted around. Dressed in a white polo shirt and khakis that stopped just short of his white tennis shoes, Alderman Porter stood in the doorway, arms folded across his chest. He was an older man, but still quite good-looking. He had thick silver hair and clear green eyes.

"Good afternoon, Alderman Porter," Lolli said, approaching him and shaking his hand.

"It was a good afternoon until Sally told me we had a party crasher," Porter replied, squeezing her hand a little too firmly. "I've got nearly thirty kids running amok across my property and the goats in the petting zoo are making short work of my Kentucky bluegrass, so let's make this quick. What can I do for you?"

"Please forgive my intrusion, sir. I have a pressing piece of business to discuss and I'm afraid it's time sensitive."

With his hand, Porter motioned for Lolli to continue.

"Well, as I'm sure you know, my father is throwing a birthday party for my mother tonight. The event is actually twofold. At the party he'll also be announcing his intention to run for Brooklyn borough president. The plan is to—"

"Let me stop you right there," Alderman Porter cut in. "I know all about Chancellor's little coming-out party. I'm going to tell you like I told your brother C.J. when he asked: I have no plans to support your father's run."

Lolli wasn't surprised. She'd heard as much from Ghost but wanted to try her hand anyhow. "May I ask why not?"

"You want the politically correct answer or the truth?"

"The truth is the only answer I would respect," Lolli said.

"Quite frankly, I just don't like your father."

Lolli knew that her father and Alderman Porter weren't besties, but she was unaware of any malice between them. "I'm afraid I don't understand, sir."

"Then let me clarify it for you. Your father is a criminal."

Lolli felt a tingle shoot up her spine. "Alderman, I wouldn't insult your intelligence by trying to deny something we both already know. My family has a less-than-pristine background, but over the last two decades my father has been working very hard to wash away some of the dirt of our forefathers."

Alderman Porter laughed. "Let's cut the bullshit, *Lollipop*. You can dress a pig in a suit but that won't make it not a pig. Your father may have everyone else fooled with his silver-lined speeches and charitable acts of kindness in the American ghettos, but I know a devil when I see one."

Lolli could've reached out and socked the alderman in the mouth, but she worked hard to keep her composure. "And here I was under the impression that you were a friend to the King family."

"I was a friend to your grandfather, Edward. He was a man who understood how things worked."

"And what's that supposed to mean?"

"Let me give you a little history lesson. When Edward King ran things, he made illegal money but he kept it under the radar and within his own community. It was easy for us to turn a blind eye to his dealings because they never overlapped with our interests. Then here comes your father with his big ideas and political ambitions. He's sticking his nose in things that don't concern him."

"I don't understand," Lolli said. "When he was up for the seat on city council, you were one of his biggest supporters."

"Because he paid me handsomely to smile and stand next to him in for a couple of photo ops. I never expected him to actually pull it off. We let him have his little victory, but now it seems he has his sights set on bigger game. If we let him get elected borough president, who knows what office he'd set his eyes on next."

Realization hit Lolli like a brick. She tiptoed toward Alderman Porter, dropping her innocent posture. "So, this is all because you think my father is going to oppose your run for mayor when the time comes?"

Porter chuckled. "He's welcome to try. Dropping off cash in greasy chicken bags might've worked in getting him on the city council, but I'm not sure how well that'll go over in a mayoral election."

Lolli ignored the insult. "My father is no threat to your political aspirations. In fact, he'd probably be more of a help than a hindrance in your mayoral bid. He has a lot of sway with minorities and that can translate to a whole lot of votes. Chancellor King is a man who understands the importance of having friends and always makes sure to take care of his own."

Porter laughed again. "How, by dropping off briefcases of money stained with the blood of innocent people? No thanks, I'll take my chances on winning the election on my own when my time comes. Now, if you'll excuse me, I've got a party to get back to."

Lolli resisted the urge to break his jaw. Instead, she simply said, "Thank you for your time." As she moved to the door, a thought struck her. She stopped and turned toward the alderman. "Can I ask you a question?"

"Sure."

"Do you love your children?"

Alderman Porter's eyes flashed with anger. "Is that supposed to be some kind of threat?"

"No sir. It's simply a question. I'm sure you love your kids more than anything, and they feel the same way about you. Your children would move heaven and earth to see you get what you want. We King children feel the same way about our father. Just some food for thought."

Porter's face turned beet red. "You got some balls coming

in here trying to muscle me, little girl! At first, I was just going to ignore the invitation to your mother's party, but I've changed my mind. I'm going to attend, eat the fancy food you provide, and gorge myself on expensive champagne until I'm too drunk to stand. Then, when your father extends his hand to me in friendship, I'm going to spit in it!"

"Be careful, Alderman," Lolli hissed. "There's power in words, and you might want to watch yours."

"And you should stay in a woman's place! I'm not some sniveling peckerwood in a suit who shits his pants at the site of a little blood. Before I lived in this big house, I came up in a cold-water flat off East Tremont. My mom fed six of us off of a welfare check that she had to fistfight with my drunken father not to take every month. Long before I walked the halls of an Ivy League university, I got my education on the streets. I don't scare easily. So you can go and tell the so-called king of Five Points that I got no problem wallowing in the mud with him if it comes to that. If anybody in my family so much as twists an ankle on a broken sidewalk, I'm going to hold him personally responsible and come at him with everything I got. I will call in every favor owed to me and rain a shitstorm of hellfire down on all you little ghetto birds in that cesspool that you call a kingdom. Am I making myself clear, Lollipop?"

Lolli smiled and edged closer to the alderman. "Crystal."

When Nefertiti heard the Porters' front door swing violently open, she looked up from the text message she was sending. Lolli was storming toward the car, her face rumpled with anger. Nefertiti thought she could make out wisps of smoke rolling over the top of her boss's head. She didn't have to ask how the meeting had gone.

"That piece-of-shit cracker muthafucka!" Lolli shouted,

slamming her fists into the back of the passenger seat. "How dare he talk to me like my name isn't Lolli King!"

"I take it he didn't go for your pitch?" Nefertiti said.

"I barely got two words out before he was dismissing me like some common washerwoman."

"I knew it was a bad idea coming down here to talk to him without getting your father's permission first."

"I'm not Ghost. I don't need to ask Daddy's permission before I take a shit!" Lolli spat.

"Well, the man said no. Maybe it's best we leave it alone, at least for now."

"You know me better than that, Nef. The good alderman and I will speak again, and the next time it'll be in a language that he better understands."

CHAPTER 7

"S o, you still need me to handle that for Uncle Chance?" Monster asked. He navigated his Mercedes G-Wagon through the thick traffic crossing the Brooklyn Bridge.

"Nah, it's already been taken care of," Ghost said from the passenger seat, not bothering to look up from his newspaper.

"I wish I could've gotten my hands on that snitching mutha-fucka. I would've made sure he died slow and painfully," Monster said. "Who did you get to handle it? One of them young boys from LES?"

"It's taken care of," Ghost responded. "That's all that really needs to be said about it."

Monster was not only Ghost's cousin but also one of his most trusted soldiers. They had done plenty of dirt together when Ghost was still in the streets. When Chance bumped Ghost into upper management, he had made it clear to his oldest boy that it was important for him to keep his hands clean. Chance wouldn't take it well if he found out that Ghost had recently executed a man on a public street. Ghost had been careful about it, but still. The less people who knew about his indiscretion, the better.

"You been kinda short all day," Monster said. "What's eat-ing you, G?"

"Nothing, man. Just got a lot to do before I get ready for this function tonight."

"Speaking of that—how come I didn't get an invitation?"

He'd never truly admit it, but Monster was in his feelings about not getting invited.

"Ain't your speed," Ghost said, flipping the page of his paper.

"What's that supposed to mean? It's a family gathering and I'm family . . . ain't I?"

"Of course you are, but there's more than meets the eye with this little shindig. My father is using my mother's birthday to get everybody together to ask for their support in his political campaign. It'll most likely be a roomful of old people in stuffed shirts, discussing things that men like us have no interests in."

"Men like *us* or men like *me*?"

Something in Monster's tone caused Ghost to close the newspaper and give his cousin his undivided attention. "Something on your heart, Cuz?"

Monster turned to look at Ghost. He thought about keeping quiet, but figured that if he wanted an answer to the question that had been nagging him, it was best that he was direct with it. "The streets are talking, dawg. Word is that Uncle Chance is about to give up his seat at the table to pursue this political shit."

"You know the streets is a two-faced bitch. Can't trust nothing she says," Ghost replied with a chuckle.

"Which is why I'm bringing it to you instead of letting my imagination run away with it."

"I thought it was my job to analyze my father's decisions, not yours."

"You and I both know that I couldn't care less about what goes on in the palace. I'm just worried about how his decision to step down is going to affect the common folk, such as myself. The King family won't lose much sleep if the streets run dry, but some of us aren't fortunate enough to have a legitimate business to fall back on."

Ghost didn't miss the dig and responded in kind: "And

whose fault is that? I'm constantly drilling it in all you niggas' heads the importance of being able to clean your money up. Shit, I even put a few of the homies through school when they wanted to go. I've extended the same opportunities to each and every man who flies under the King banner, but how many have taken advantage of it? The problem with most of y'all is that if it doesn't get you high, suck dick, or look good on Instagram, y'all ain't interested."

"Not everybody is as skilled as you at wearing two faces," Monster capped.

"Fuck you mean by that?"

"Meaning how you can dance between a roomful of sweet-talking white people and a group of killers and not miss a beat. I don't mean no disrespect either. All I'm saying is that whatever move Uncle Chance makes, I don't wanna be one of the niggas left out in the cold."

"Cuz, how long we been running together?"

"Since we were punk kids."

"And have I ever seen you go without?"

"Nah, Ghost. You always made sure I was in position to earn my keep."

"And that will never change. Regardless of which way my father swings on all this, I'm gonna always make sure you're well fed."

"Teach a man to fish," Monster muttered, but Ghost missed it.

The rest of the ride into Brooklyn was spent in relative silence. Every so often Monster flashed Ghost a look, but Ghost was too focused on whatever was running through his mind to notice. He had a million and one things to do before the party, and still more to do afterward. In truth, coming all the way to Brooklyn to solve Christian's problem was cutting into time that Ghost really didn't have to spare. In the end, though, showing up to this next meeting would be worth it. Helping his young protégé close this deal would be crucial to what Ghost was planning for the future.

They finally arrived at their destination, a small restaurant a few blocks from the Brooklyn Navy Yard. The windows were all boarded up due to the renovations that were supposed to be going on, before the landlord had forced them to stop working. Things had been fine when the owner of the building thought Ghost would be the tenant, but that changed when he found out that it would be Christian instead. When Christian had shown up with the bank check, expecting to sign the lease, he was unexpectedly turned away. The landlord refused to sign the lease until Ghost came to see him personally. From what Ghost understood, it had something to do with Christian's *eccentricities*, but Ghost reasoned it was likely a play for more money. Well, if this dude thought he could hustle Ghost, he had another thing coming.

"Fucking Tinkerbell," Monster grumbled under his breath when he saw Christian standing out in front of the spot waiting for them.

"Be easy, Cuz," Ghost urged.

Monster had never cared for Christian and made no attempts to hide it. Ghost couldn't tell if this was due to the fact that Christian and Ghost were so close or because Christian carried himself more flamboyantly than any of his other associates.

Christian was dressed in slim-fitting black slacks that stopped just above his bare ankles. Gold shoes studded with colorful stones adorned his feet and he wore a metallic gold jacket over a black turtleneck. He tapped his foot impatiently under a large black umbrella even though there were no signs of rain. To some, his wardrobe might've been considered a little out there, but Ghost knew that Christian had actually toned it down for today. He had seen the man wear some very question-able outfits, so he knew how different his style could be. Ghost once attended a party Christian hosted, where he dressed in full cape and crotchless pants. Compared to some of the other men Ghost kept on retainer, Christian didn't look like much in the way of a threat, but he had a particular skill set that had proven invaluable. People often underestimated the kid based on his sexual fluidity, though Christian hadn't been dubbed the Prince of the Night for no reason.

"So long as he doesn't try and sprinkle me with any of that fairy dust, we're Gucci," Monster told Ghost.

"Top of the morning, boss man," Christian greeted Ghost. "Sorry to make you come all the way to Brooklyn when I know your plate is full today, but your friend is being incredi-bly unreasonable."

"Let's just get this shit wrapped up so I can be on my way," Ghost said as he stepped through the doors.

Christian moved to the side to let Monster pass next, but the big man deferred, giving Christian a mock bow. "After you."

Christian rolled his eyes and followed Ghost inside.

In the lobby, seated at a plastic table, was the pain-in-the-ass landlord, Hamid Rusa. He was flanked by his brothers and business partners, Pitel and Felix. Hamid was a portly Pakistani man with a pencil-thin mustache and dark hair that had begun to thin on top. Several gold chains hung around his neck, tick-ling the curly black chest hairs that peeked through the top of his unbuttoned blue shirt. When he saw Ghost, he stood and flashed a smile that revealed the teeth of a man who smoked too many cigarettes and drank too much coffee.

"If it isn't the prince of Five Points," Hamid said in his thick accent. "I am honored that you were able to join us this fine morning."

"Cut the bullshit, Hamid, and tell me what the fuck the problem is."

"The problem is you weren't honest with me about your intentions for this place when I agreed to lease it to you," Hamid said.

"What are you talking about? I told you that I was looking to turn it into a nightclub."

"What kind of nightclub are you planning to open that requires these?" Hamid motioned to Felix, who stepped forward with a long cardboard box. When Hamid popped it open, Ghost saw several chains attached to leather straps. "We came in here the other day and found these hanging from the ceiling. It took us nearly an hour to take them all down."

"Which you had no right to do," Christian cut in. "You've got no say so as to what goes on in my spot!"

"Don't you mean *my* spot that you are hoping to lease?" Hamid countered. "I have plenty of say over what happens in this building and I don't think I like what you're trying to turn it into."

"What I'm trying to turn it into is a cash cow, but you're trying to put shit on my game!" Christian shot back.

Ghost watched in amusement as the two men went back and forth. Christian very rarely lost his composure, but Ghost could see that Hamid was doing a good job of pushing his buttons. Part of him wanted to let it continue, to see what would happen when Hamid finally pushed too far. It would certainly be entertaining, yet it would also further damage a relationship that he needed to work.

"All right," Ghost finally interjected, "Hamid, when we sat down you agreed to let us lease this place with no questions asked, so long as we agreed to kick you six months' rent in advance. What goes on inside of this place shouldn't be your concern, so long as you get your money—money that Christian tried to pay you and you refused, for reasons that I'm still trying to understand. So why don't you stop with the fucking games and tell me what the real problem is?"

Hamid excused himself and fell into a huddle with his brothers. They engaged in a quiet debate in a language that Ghost couldn't understand. After a minute or so, they broke apart and Hamid turned his attention back to Ghost.

"Ghost, you've always been straight up. You're solid, so I can fuck with you."

"But?"

Hamid cast an uneasy glance back at his brothers, who motioned for him to continue. "This business with your friend isn't going to work. I don't care for the crowd that he's going to attract."

"And what kind of crowd is that?" Christian asked. "Other than scores of beautiful people willing to pay for what they want."

Hamid was hesitant. He looked to Ghost as if waiting for his approval to say what was on his mind. Ghost nodded. "Faggots," Hamid said. "No disrespect, because I don't care if you suck dick or not. It's just that attracting that type of crowd to this neighborhood would be bad for business. My neighbors won't appreciate having an establishment that caters to carnal things."

Ghost shook his head at this small-minded view. "Hamid, let's try and be reasonable about this."

"I am being reasonable, Ghost. That's why I wanted to meet—so I could tell you personally, instead of just killing the whole deal outright. If you had been looking to open anything else in this space, I wouldn't have a problem with it, but for the type of club your friend is trying to open, I can't do it."

"This is some bullshit," Christian blurted out. "I've already paid for the permits and advanced the carpenters half their money for the renovations. What am I supposed to do now?"

"Maybe you can take what's owed to you in trade?" Pitel said, cupping his hand to his mouth and flicking his tongue along his cheek to simulate a blow job.

"Or maybe I'll take it in blood," Christian said. The sweetness in his voice had turned icy and harsh.

Sensing the threat, Felix, who was the more menacing of the brothers, stepped forward. "You've got a sharp tongue. Maybe I should curve it for you?" He reached out to touch Christian's face, but immediately found his wrist clasped in the smaller man's hand.

Christian's eyes flickered sinisterly as he applied pressure. "Honey, you're about to find out that my tongue isn't the only thing that's sharp," he said in a near whisper. Then he jammed the point of his umbrella through Felix's foot, pinning it to the floor.

Pitel moved to help his brother, but Christian had something for him too. He withdrew the umbrella from Felix's foot and wielded it like a club, smashing the handle across Pitel's nose. Seeing his brothers get the business, Hamid lurched toward Christian, who was pouncing from brother to brother, whacking them about the head and back with the umbrella, issuing several nonlethal cuts with its tip. Had he wanted to, he could've killed all three brothers with the umbrella, but this fight wasn't about killing—it was about teaching a lesson, and Christian took the boys to school.

"Christ, G!" Monster shouted. "Shouldn't we do something?"

"Like what?" Ghost moved his foot to avoid the blood flecking the floor. "I think he's got it under control."

By the time Christian finished, Hamid had not only signed

the lease but also agreed to knock off two months of rent. (That had been Ghost's idea, for all the trouble Hamid had put them through.) Only when the paperwork was signed and the chains were rehung from the ceiling did Christian allow the brothers to seek medical attention.

"I gotta admit," Monster said once he and Ghost were back in the car, "I've got a whole new respect for that little twinkling muthafucka. I didn't think he had it in him."

"They never do," Ghost said proudly. "Let's get out of here. We've got one more stop to make."

"You got another mess to clean up?"

"Nah, this time we're going to *make* one."

PART II

I'VE BEEN TO MANY PLACES, BUT I'M BROOKLYN'S OWN

CHAPTER 8

F resh half listened to the radio as he walked into his bedroom. "Good morning, New York City!" announced the disc jockey. "It's eight a.m. and already a crisp fifty-eight degrees, with highs expected to reach somewhere in the seventies. It's going to be a beautiful day in the Rotten Apple, so get out and make the best of it!"

Fresh had been up for about two hours. He had never been the type to sleep for more than a few hours at a time, crashing just long enough to ensure that he was functional throughout the day. He was too afraid that he would miss something while he was sleeping, especially the opportunity to make a dollar. As a kid, his dad often repeated a mantra: *A resting man is either rich enough to afford to rest or a poor man who lacks the motivation to change his circumstances. If you're sleeping, you're not earning.* It was not just the most important jewel his old man had ever dropped on him but the *only* one. Fresh's sperm donor had walked out on his family when he was still very young, leaving his mother to raise him and his older brother on her own.

Fresh was dressed in a towel, flip-flops, and a do-rag, his skin still drying from the shower. He paused in front of the smudged mirror stationed atop his old wooden dresser. He was a handsome kid—rich brown skin, chestnut eyes, and thick pink lips that he kept moisturized. With the patience of a doctor removing the bandages from a burn victim, he unwrapped his do-rag. A lot of cats in the hood had waves, but none had them like Fresh. He kept his hair tapered on the sides and in the back, but let the top grow a little thicker, and it ran over his head in waves that could've sunk the *Titanic* a second time. He ran his index finger and thumb over the thin goatee that he had been trying to grow since freshman year. *Soon*, he thought to himself, praying that the beard gods would one day bless him.

Moving to his bed, where his outfit for the day was laid out, Fresh pulled on a pair of dark-blue jeans and a white polo shirt, which he had spent a good ten minutes ironing the night before. The collar was starched and pressed to a point so fine that Fresh could have cut himself if he wasn't careful. He'd earned the moniker Fresh because he was the kind of cat who could take some low-end merch and mix it with some high-end drip and convince the world he was worth a million dollars, even if he held less than one hundred dollars in pocket. Life was a stage and he fancied himself the star of the show.

He grabbed his wallet plus the $163 he'd left on his nightstand and shoved them into his pockets. On his way out, he snatched the gold chain he kept hanging on the frame of his mirror. It was a decent-sized link chain, with a pendant on the end that held an old picture of him with his mom, older brother, and little sister. It was from Easter, when their mother forced them to deck out in their Sunday best. It was the last year his mother made them dress up. It was the year when things had changed.

Fresh found his little sister, Crissy, sitting at the table hunched over a bowl of cereal and scrolling her cell phone. She was a beautiful young girl with thick black hair and skin the color of unprocessed chocolate. She normally wore her hair in braids, but that morning she had pulled it into two Afro puffs.

"What up, big head?" Fresh tugged at one of her puffs.

"Quit it, ugly." Crissy sucked her teeth and checked to make sure he hadn't messed up her hair.

"Where's Mommy?" Fresh asked as he was rummaging through the refrigerator. He wasn't hungry, it was just something he did out of habit whenever he was in the kitchen. The shelves were looking light and somebody would have to procure some food soon.

"I'm not sure if she's come in yet," Crissy said. "She told me she was going to pick up some extra hours at the hospital. Didn't you read the group text she sent us?"

Fresh's silence said that he hadn't. Crissy shook her head.

"What time did *you* get in last night?" she asked. Crissy was thirteen, but carried herself like she was much older. Her mother insisted that she had been here, on earth, before this lifetime.

"None of your business," he mumbled. He didn't feel like being pressed by his baby sister.

"It's going to be my business when Mommy insists that I give her a report on what went on in this house while she was gone."

"Why don't you just tell her that I was here all night?"

"Because she'd know it was a lie," Crissy said with a twinge of sass. "You've never been able to sit in one place for too long. Besides, when she called me last night and asked where you were, I said you had stepped out. I didn't expect you to come creeping in during the wee hours."

"I'm a grown-ass man out here," Fresh capped. "I don't have to account for my comings and goings to nobody, not for you or Mommy."

"Is that right?"

Their mother, Irene, appeared in the doorway as if out of thin air. She was wearing black slacks and a blue shirt with an IHOP logo on the breast. Irene looked like an older version of

Crissy, except she was thicker and wore her hair in a natural cut.

"Oh, hey Ma. I thought you were still at work," Fresh said, planting a kiss on her cheek.

"I was. I came in about five this morning," Irene said. "Had just enough time to catch a few hours of sleep and shower. Now I have to go to my other job."

"Gosh, Ma, you're going to work yourself to death. Why don't you slow down and rest?" Fresh hated seeing his mother slave at multiple jobs.

"*Chile*, these bills don't care if I'm tired or not. They still have to be paid."

"You know I could help out. Take some time off from school and—"

"Absolutely not. It's not your job to tend this house. Your responsibilities are to keep yourself and your sister out of trouble, then finish school. I know that half the time your ass doesn't show up or leaves early, but your grades are still good enough for you to graduate. All you've got to do is hold on for a few more months."

"I can quit and get a GED. That would save me some time."

"I said no, Frederick," Irene responded, calling him by his given name to let him know that she was serious. "In this house, we walk that stage. I graduated from high school. Even your brother Kevin managed to get his diploma, may he rest in peace."

Kevin was Fresh's older brother. Crissy had a different dad than the two of them. Before her dad came along and got Irene pregnant, it had just been Irene and her two sons. Fresh was the hustler of the family, but Kevin had been a gangster. He used to run with Ghost King and rumor had it that Kevin had even dropped a few bodies. He was a feared man on the streets, which was eventually what got him killed. A girl he'd been seeing on the side had gotten into a physical altercation with the father of one of her kids. She threatened that she was going to get Kevin to come see him. It was an empty threat because Kevin wasn't the type to get into altercations over pussy, especially when it didn't belong to him in the first place. But his girl's ex didn't know this. The coward walked up behind Kevin one night and shot him in the back. He lost his life and never even knew why.

"I gotta get ready to get out of here," Irene said, casting a glance at her watch. "I should be off in time to come home and make dinner, but in the event that I'm not, there's twenty dollars on the coffee table. That should be enough to get you guys some McDonald's." She kissed Crissy then Fresh. "I need you to walk your sister to the bus stop this morning, Frederick."

"Ma, I'm not a baby," Crissy pouted. "I can walk to the bus stop with my friends like I normally do." She had planned on meeting up with her crew so she could get the gossip about yesterday's fight at school.

"Not today, honey. I hear a girl about your age got snatched in the projects the other day. My heart can't take losing another child, so just humor me for today. Okay?"

"Yes ma'am."

"Don't worry, Mommy," Fresh said. "Even if somebody was to snatch Crissy, they'd probably give her back the same day."

"That's not funny," Irene said. "Now, walk me to the elevator. I've got a bone to pick with you."

As soon as Irene's back was turned, Crissy stuck her tongue out at Fresh; he responded by waving his fist.

With his head hung like a kid being called to the principal's office, Fresh followed his mother into the hallway. "What's up, Ma?"

Irene gave a cautious look around before dipping her hand into her purse and pulling out a wad of neatly folded money. "What is this?" she asked him.

Fresh shrugged. "Looks like money."

"Boy, don't get cute. I know what it is. I wanna know where it came from. It mysteriously appeared in my sock drawer."

"Looks like the Lord done blessed you," Fresh said, flashing a toothy grin.

"Frederick, how many times am I gonna have to get on you about throwing stones at the penitentiary?"

"I ain't out throwing stones at nothing. I just got a little hustle that I do from time to time for some extra cash. Nothing that can get me in any trouble, though."

"Boy, anything you're out there doing for money that doesn't come with a W-2 can get you in trouble. I'm not stupid. I know what's going on out there with those guys you hang around with. You're not a baby anymore. I can't be running behind you trying to chase you off the block. You're a young man and have to make your own decisions. I just hope you make the right ones. Do you understand?"

Fresh nodded.

The elevator pinged and the door slid open.

"Okay, let me get out of here and get to work." Irene stepped into the elevator. "Remember what I told you, Frederick."

"I will." As the door started to close, Fresh stuck his hand out to stop it. "So, since you don't agree with how I make my money, does that mean you're going to give it back?"

"Boy, please. I haven't had my hair done in weeks, and a pedicure longer still. Mama is about to get her life. Thanks, son." She winked as the door slammed shut.

"What did Mommy wanna talk to you about?" Crissy asked as

she and Fresh walked up the avenue toward the bus stop.

"Ma's just being Ma. Nothing for you to worry about," Fresh said. "You got money on you?"

"I have like four bucks left from my chore money."

Fresh reached into his pocket and peeled off a twenty from his wad of cash. "Take that."

"Thanks," Crissy said, stuffing the bill in her pocket. "You know, you don't always have to give me money. I know you ain't got it like that."

"Let your mother tell it, I'm a kingpin," Fresh joked.

"You can't blame her for being a little worried, especially after what happened to Kevin."

"I'm not out here heavy like Kevin was. I'm just hustling here and there, nothing too crazy." Fresh sold drugs from time to time, but he wasn't on the block every day with it like some of the other guys, including his friend Pain. Fresh was a man of multiple hustles, with drug dealing being his least favorite. It was too time-consuming; Fresh preferred instant gratification.

"That makes it even worse," Chrissy said.

"How do you mean?"

"When I decided that I wanted to play basketball and didn't make the team the first time, you told me that it was because my heart wasn't in it. You said that anything I wanted to be great at, I should be all in with it. Same rules apply to you out here hustling. If you're not all in, then what's the point?"

A smile touched Fresh's lips. "You know, sometimes you're too smart for your own good."

To get from their building to the bus stop, they had to walk north on Nostrand Avenue. Nostrand was a notorious strip always jumping with illicit activity. Normally, Fresh spent his time there with the rest of his knucklehead friends, but he hadn't been up that way in a few days. A kid had gotten shot a few nights before so the strip was hot. But because it was early in the morning, most of the people out and about were headed to school or work. On the corner, though, Fresh ran into some boys posted up. He gave daps to a couple of the dudes he knew.

"Let me get a bone, Fresh," said one of the boys.

Fresh fished around in his pocket and pulled out an empty pack. It was then he remembered that he had smoked his last cigarette when he came in the night before. Since the store was right there he decided to run in and get a fresh pack. "You want anything from out of here?" he asked Crissy.

"Just some chips or something. And please don't take too long. I don't want to miss the bus."

Fresh grabbed a bottle of water from the bodega's cooler, then snatched two bags of sour cream and onion chips for Crissy. He was at the counter getting his cigarettes and paying for his purchase when something drew his attention to the store's window. A shiny black BMW idled along the curb and all the corner boys immediately clustered around it. Fresh didn't recognize the car. He probably wouldn't have paid it any mind if he hadn't noticed Crissy leaning into the window talking to the driver. He tossed twenty dollars on the counter and didn't bother waiting for his change before making hurried steps back outside. When he saw who was driving the vehicle, anger rose to his chest.

Malice was just as his name suggested—someone with the intent or desire to do evil. Originally from the Fort Greene projects, he had migrated to Fresh's neighborhood a few years back. He was the right-hand man of a dude named Vick who used to run the neighborhood. When Vick got locked up, Malice slid into his position and had held it ever since. Most of the dudes in Fresh's area either hustled for Malice or bought their drugs from him. He was the man in their hood, but Fresh couldn't stand him. It wasn't that Malice had ever done anything to him directly, but his energy rubbed Fresh the wrong way. Now, here was this slimy muthafucka whispering to his baby sister like a snake charmer.

"Crissy!" Fresh barked her name so sharply that the girl jumped. "Let's go!"

"A'ight, gosh. Why you gotta be yelling all crazy?" Crissy said, trying to hide her embarrassment. When she reached her brother, he gave her a little shove for good measure.

"Don't be out here hanging into no damn car window like a hood rat," Fresh said through gritted teeth.

"Yo, why don't you ease up, shorty. It wasn't even like that," Malice said from the car window. Fresh ignored him, but then he heard the door open and a boot hit the curb. Fresh turned to see Malice emerging from his whip. An average-sized dude with a growing beer gut he hid beneath baggy shirts, Malice wore a thick gold chain around his neck, the weight of it swinging like a pendulum as he moved toward the siblings. "We was just talking."

"She's thirteen and don't need to be out here in no grown-ass men's faces," Fresh told him, trying to keep his voice even. He knew it wouldn't take too much to get Malice started, which is what he was hoping to avoid.

Malice gave Crissy a lecherous once-over. "Shit, I thought she was pushing at least seventeen. You better keep your good eye on this one, Fresh."

"I'll take your advice, thanks," Fresh said sarcastically before walking off.

"Have a good day at school, lil' mama," Malice called after them. When Fresh looked back he saw Malice adjusting his crotch and looking at his sister like she was a piece of meat.

"Don't let me catch you all up in that nigga's face again," Fresh said when they were down the block.

"I wasn't all up in anybody's face. I told him that I liked his car, so he was showing me the inside." To Crissy, the whole thing was innocent.

"I'll bet that wasn't all he was trying to show you. Dudes like Malice ain't no good. All they want is one thing."

"The same thing you get from the three or four girls per week you sneak in and out of your room?"

"The difference is that I'm grown and you're thirteen! Crissy, I know you think I'm just trying to boss you around on some big-brother shit, but I'm only trying to protect you. I'm not stupid enough to think you haven't discovered the opposite sex yet, and that's cool, but you gotta be smart about the kind of guys you allow into your space. You're young, pretty, and smart, so you're gonna be a magnet for wolves. I'm trying to make sure you're wise enough to know a predator when you see one, because my baby sister ain't gonna end up anybody's prey. You feel me?"

"I guess," Crissy muttered. She understood what her brother was saying, but his delivery was too harsh.

Five minutes later, the bus showed up and it was time for them to part ways. Crissy fell in step with two of her friends who had just arrived at the bus stop.

"Crissy," Fresh called after her. When she turned he told her, "I love you."

She smiled at her older brother and got on the bus with her friends. Crissy was a pain in the ass, but Fresh loved her with everything he had. She was the one person, besides his mom, who he would do anything for . . . anything at all.

When Fresh came back down the avenue, everyone was still pretty much where he'd left them, including Malice, who was sitting on the hood of his car, rolling a blunt. Fresh was tempted to run down on him and knock the shit out of him, but that would likely create a problem he didn't need. He decided to let Malice's little stunt earlier slide and continue about his day. As he got closer, though, Malice noticed him. He tapped one of his henchmen on the shoulder and nodded at Fresh, then whispered something that caused the henchman to chuckle. Fresh wasn't dumb. He knew that Malice was trying to bait him but he had no intention of feeding into the bullshit. Until the gangster opened his mouth.

"What up, Fresh? You still in your feelings?"

"Nah, we good, fam," Fresh replied.

"Oh, a'ight," said Malice, "I should hope so, because you're one of the few lil' niggas from over this side that I actually fuck with. You stick to your own and don't get involved in other people's bullshit. I respect that."

"Thanks."

"So, I'm saying, when you gonna come fuck with me and get this money?"

"Thanks, but I'm cool. Me and my people kinda got our own thing going."

"What? Them little g-packs and ready rock you be hustling by the projects?" Malice said. "That's sneaker money, man. I'm talking about the kind of cake that'll keep you off the bus and riding in style like me." He ran his hand over the hood of the BMW.

"I see you out here shining and I respect your hustle, but I'm cool with grinding for mine," Fresh said.

"Shorty, that ain't no grind, that's a rub!" Malice laughed. "Look, I ain't gonna twist your arm to make no paper. I was just trying to offer you an opportunity to fill some of those holes in your pocket. You can buy something nice for that pretty little sister of yours."

"On some real shit, you need to keep my sister out your mouth."

The boys on the corner must've sensed Fresh's anger, because those loyal to Malice began closing ranks around him.

"Nah, you ain't gotta worry about your sister in my mouth. In a year or two? Maybe, but not right now."

"You need to watch your fucking mouth," Fresh said evenly, taking a step toward him. He stopped when Malice lifted his shirt and showed him the butt of a gun jammed down the front of his pants.

"Or what?" Malice challenged. Fresh was silent. "Just like I thought. You be walking around out here with your nose in the air because your brother's name used to ring, but yours don't. Kevin was about that life, but you ain't no gangster."

"He might not be a gangster, but he rolls with a few," chimed Pain, who had just appeared at the curb. He was wearing a tattered fatigue jacket, black Timbs, and baggy blue jeans. His short Afro hadn't been combed in a day or two, still sporting traces of lint from wherever he had slept the night before. His dark eyes were fixed on Malice. "What's good?" he said.

"What's good is that I offered your man my hand in friendship and he spat in it," Malice answered.

"So, this is what friendship looks like where you're from?" Pain glanced over the boys who had now surrounded Fresh. Something in his gaze made a few of them take a cautious step back. "I'd say it looks like you're planning on an ass-whipping."

"What if I am?" Malice said.

Pain shrugged. "I ain't got no issue with that, if you're looking to have a fair one with Fresh. Now, if y'all were thinking about jumping one of my closest friends, then it might become something else." He flicked his tongue ever so slightly so that Malice could see the razor resting on it. It was a trick Pain had mastered during the few months he had spent on Rikers Island.

"You ain't never heard the expression about bringing a knife to a gunfight?" Malice adjusted his gun.

Pain let his eyes roam from the gun back to Malice's face. His expression remained cool. "Indeed I have, which is why I'm hoping we can end this without me or my boy going to the morgue and you or one of yours ending up in the ER trying to get your face stapled back on." Pain waved his hands in front of his face like a magician. Two razors appeared in his hands, small but sharp. "We might be few, but we're crazy. You trying to put that to the test?"

Malice appeared to be weighing his options. He was a shooter, but he knew that the young man standing between him and Fresh was a gladiator. Pain was one of the younger dudes in the neighborhood who the older guys respected—he had the heart of a lion. He wasn't the type to back down from a fight under any circumstances, even the threat of being shot. If you did happen to get the best of Pain, then you had better grow eyes in the back of your head because he was going to keep coming back until you were dead.

Malice knew he needed to bow out of the situation gracefully, so he was pleased when a silver Mercedes pulled up to the curb.

"We'll dance another time," Pain told Malice before heading over to the Benz.

Fresh followed Pain and then gave him a dap.

"Thanks, man," he said.

"You know how we do, kid," Pain chanted, returning his blades to their hiding spots. "What did you do to piss Malice off so early in the morning?"

"It's a long story. But yo, who's in the Benz?" Fresh asked. Everyone on the block seemed to be flocking around it.

Pain cracked a half smile. "If you'd checked the text message I sent you this morning, you would know."

CHAPTER 9

By the time Shadow pushed his mother's car into Brooklyn, rush hour had started to thicken. Normally, when he came into the city, he used public transportation or spent a grip on Ubers. But on those rare occasions when he was allowed to drive, he was thrown the keys to one of his family's low-end hoopties. Driving the luxury Mercedes was a whole different experience. It was empowering.

He had some time to kill, so he took the long way to the hood and detoured through downtown. He rode slowly up Fulton, absorbing the sights and sounds. Stores were just rolling up their gates to open for the day's business. To his left loomed the Albee Square Mall, a Brooklyn landmark that brought back a storm of memories. As a kid his father would bring him here to shop, regaling him with stories of the brazen capers he and his friends pulled in the area before he had gotten his act together.

Though the power base of the King family was Five Points, it was Brooklyn where Chance King had put down his family's roots. Shadow was young when they left Brooklyn but old enough to remember the leaner times they'd spent as residents of Kings County. Back then, his dad still had one leg knee-deep in the game. Sure, he did the real estate thing, but he hadn't really started making life-changing money from it. The family had occupied the top floor of a walk-up apartment building in Bedford-Stuyvesant, on a not-so-nice block. There were some tough cats in his old neighborhood, but they all respected

Chance King. When the family finally got their weight up and moved out of the neighborhood, Chance purchased the building they once lived in. He rented out the other units, but kept the top-floor apartment. His dad always said that it would serve as a reminder of his humble beginnings.

For Shadow, it was a crash pad. Unbeknownst to his dad, he'd had a set of keys made to the place. Sometimes when he was in the hood, he would slide through the old apartment, especially on days when it was too cold for him and his friends to smoke weed outside or if he was trying to bang a girl. Sometimes he would sit in the window of that apartment and stare out at the neighborhood, imagining what it was like to see it through his father's eyes.

The deeper he ventured into Brooklyn, the more the scenery changed. The fancy shops and open-air eateries dissipated, and soon the streets were lined with bodegas, liquor stores, and Chinese restaurants. This is when Shadow slipped into character: the driver's seat went back a little farther, the music went up a little louder, and he configured his face to look a little harder. He was in the jungle now. If you appeared weak, you were fair game.

He spotted a familiar face at a bus stop on Nostrand Avenue, locked in a heated discussion with a young girl. Shadow hit the horn, but his friend was so preoccupied that he didn't turn around. He wanted to pull over, but there was too much traffic. Circling the block was too much of a pain; he didn't want to drive a few extra blocks just to make the turn that would allow him to come back around on that side of the street.

"Fuck it," Shadow said, and kept moving. When he stopped at the next red light, he noticed a person with a familiar walk coming up the block, headed for the train station. She was wearing a long black wig, overcoat, and dark glasses, but Shadow didn't have to see her face to know who it was. He'd recognize that gait anywhere. It was the stride of a panther looking for a kill. The light had barely turned green before Shadow sped through it and bent around the corner. He pulled up next to a fire hydrant and threw on the hazards before hoping out. He was leery of leaving the car there for too long because the thirsty-ass meter maids were always lurking, so he had to make this quick. If he didn't catch her before she went down into the station, there was no telling when he'd bump into her again. With this in mind, he broke into a jog. She was just about to descend the train station steps and out of sight when she heard him.

"Hey, pretty girl!" Shadow called out, with his hands cupped around his mouth like a bullhorn. She never broke her stride. Dudes probably shouted corny lines at her all day to get her attention. Shadow had to get creative or risk losing her again. "Your mama still make the best griot in the hood?" At the mention of one of her mother's specialty dishes, she stopped in her tracks.

The woman turned, looking over the rim of her sunglasses. There was only one person she knew who loved her mother's griot enough to be in the streets shouting about it. A scowl touched her lips. "It must be snowing in hell if the crown prince of the King monarchy is out here crawling through the slums," she scoffed, folding her arms over her breasts.

Her reception was colder than he'd expected, but not as cold as it could've been. They had history, not all of it good. "Voodoo, how can you wound me by saying such a thing?" he said, placing his hand dramatically over his heart.

"Wound you? Shadow, you're lucky I didn't pop you." She jiggled her bag to suggest that she was carrying. He expected nothing less from her. "What are you doing out here this morning? Trolling for schoolgirls?"

"See, now you're just out of pocket with the insults. I know we haven't seen each other in a minute, but—"

"Is it that simple to you?" Voodoo cut him off. "We haven't seen each other *in a minute?* And why is that, Shadow? Or is that selective memory of yours kicking in and you only remember stations that paint you as an angel instead of the devil I know you to be?"

Shadow couldn't blame Voodoo for going in on him. Their relationship used to be rock-solid, at least until Shadow cracked the foundation. As little kids, they grew up on the same block and Shadow was smitten with Voodoo from the first time he saw her sitting on the stoop with Lolli, sharing a pack of chocolate chip cookies. Whenever she played with his sister, Shadow made sure he was around. And the days that she didn't come over, he would sit on the stoop all day hoping to catch a glimpse of her.

Of course, Maureen didn't approve of Shadow's infatuation with Voodoo. Though they were from the same block, Maureen thought the girl's pedigree disqualified her from dating her baby boy. Voodoo was from a poor Haitian family, dressed in hand-me-down clothes, and spoke with a thick accent, which wore down with time. Maureen looked at everything like a business arrangement, including who her children dated; neither Voodoo nor her family had anything to offer the Kings. But Maureen's disapproval didn't stop Shadow in his pursuit.

Shadow and Voodoo started out by humping on the playground and eventually graduated to giving each other their virginity. (Shadow wasn't a virgin, actually, but he let her believe he was.) Even when the Kings moved out of the hood, Shadow and Voodoo continued to see each other. It was never anything official, but they held special places in each other's hearts. Until Shadow broke hers.

One night, Shadow and some of his white friends from high school were at a college party at Temple University, getting wasted. It was his first and last time experimenting with molly. At the party, he ran into a girl from his old neighborhood. He only knew her by her face, but it was her ass that had his attention that night. One thing led to another and soon Shadow had her bent over a laundry hamper in one of the bathrooms digging for gold in her pussy. Shadow and Voodoo weren't exclusive, but he was still wrong for sleeping with a girl from their neighborhood. It had been too close to home, yet his drugged-out brain told him that since he'd done it in another state, it didn't count. Besides, with the girl going to school all the way in Philadelphia, at least a hundred miles from Brooklyn, there was no way that Voodoo would ever find out—right?

It took only a week for shit to hit the fan. Apparently, the girl had taken offense to Shadow ghosting her after getting the goodies, so she started running her mouth to her friends back in Brooklyn about her sexual escapade with the prince of Five Points. She even gassed it up, making it seem like it was some ongoing thing, instead of him just smashing and then dismissing her. Word eventually got back to Voodoo, which led to her and two of her homegirls taking the ride down to Philly and beating the dog shit out of the girl on campus. Voodoo almost went to jail over that.

Shadow had avoided Voodoo for a week after he got word of what went down, but he couldn't duck her forever. When she finally confronted him, his first reaction was to lie. He tried spinning some story about the girl trying to fuck him and him shooting her down. He was such a convincing liar that had it been anybody other than Voodoo, he might've successfully convinced her. Alas, just as he knew Voodoo's heart, she knew his and saw right through the lie. That night, they parted over hostile words; it was the last time they'd spoken. Had Shadow been thinking, he'd have just accepted responsibility for what he'd done and apologized to Voodoo, but his ego wouldn't allow it. He was a King. By the time his heart started to ache from missing her and he reached out in reconciliation, it was too late. Voodoo had blocked his number and he was too much of a player to try to call her from a different phone. The last he'd heard, Voodoo had moved out of her parents' apartment. He had the resources to track her down if he wanted to, but he'd let it be. He'd heard through the grapevine that she'd moved into a loft somewhere in Williamsburg and was dating a square dude who worked at a bank.

"You still on that, huh?" Shadow rediscovered his voice. "Can't get over what happened?"

"I'm never *not* going to be on that," Voodoo replied. "That shit was foul, Shadow."

"Yeah, it was," he said. "What I did to you was fucked up on so many levels that even now I'm still not really sure what to say."

"You can start with an apology."

"I'm sorry."

"And that's all I ever wanted. It's just too bad it took you this long to say it to me."

"What is time to two people who exist in their own space?" he said, reaching for her hand, which she pulled away.

"I stopped being the stars to your moon when you let the next bitch plant her flag," Voodoo said, doing a poor job of masking the emotions in her voice. "I'm not trying to be rude, but I got somewhere to be."

"What? That new nigga you fucking got you on a schedule?"

"I see you're still the same old Shadow, worried about everything except what's important. Not that it's any of your business, but I don't want to be late for work."

"You got a job?" Shadow said with a chuckle. For as long as he'd known Voodoo, she always had a hustle, but never a *job*. "What happened to the pact we made as kids to never have to work to make the next man rich?"

"That pact, like most of the other silly shit I believed in, went out the window when I found myself by myself. Some of us don't have wealthy relatives to fall back on."

"That's an easy fix. All you have to do is agree to be mine for all time," Shadow said, extending his hand.

Voodoo looked at his hand. For as much as she wanted to take it, she knew she couldn't. "You and I both know your mother ain't trying to hear that. Maybe that's the real reason you fucked that girl—because she's got an education and I don't. I know how the Kings feel about breeding and I don't fit that mold."

"They broke the mold after they made you," Shadow responded.

"Oh, of this I am absolutely sure. They don't build bitches like me anymore and they probably won't anytime soon. Still, for all that I bring to the table, it wasn't enough to satisfy you."

"Don't blame yourself for my greedy nature."

"I wouldn't and I don't," she said. "Not seeing a real queen when she was kneeling right in front of you was your bad, not mine, Your Highness. In the end your trash turned out to be someone else's treasure, and for that I thank you. Take care of yourself, Shadow." She started heading down the stairs into the train station.

"This is how we're gonna leave it? You're never gonna talk to me again?" Shadow called after her.

Voodoo stopped and turned back to him. "After the way you did me? I'll never reach out to you, but who knows? I may decide to unblock your number one of these days. It'll be up to you to keep calling and see if I did or not."

"Damn, that's cold, Voodoo."

"Nah, lil' nigga. That's *not* cold, it's game." Voodoo disappeared into the train station.

Shadow waited until she was out of sight before letting a smile spread across his face. He had been skeptical about approaching her because he wasn't sure what type of reception he would get. She handled him cold as hell, but the fact that she didn't spit in his face and storm off meant that all wasn't lost. Now he had a difficult decision to make: how long should he wait before blowing up her phone? He was without question going to call. He wanted that old thing back.

CHAPTER 10

B y the time Shadow made it around the block and back to the avenue, Fresh was no longer at the bus stop. He spotted him in a thicket of hooligans in front of a bodega. His childhood friend was talking to a dude who Shadow knew by the name of Malice. Shadow knew what kind of man Malice was, and he also knew what kind of man Fresh wasn't, so to see the two of them chatting raised an eyebrow. From Fresh's body language, Shadow figured the conversation wasn't friendly. When he saw Malice lift his shirt to flash something, he realized exactly how unfriendly it was.

Keeping his eye on the group of young men and one hand on the wheel, Shadow punched in a code on the radio dial (which his parents didn't think he knew). The radio flashed twice as if it was about to power off and a secret compartment dropped down from under the glove box. Inside was a small derringer. It was his mother's gun and held only two shots, but they'd have to be enough. Shadow didn't want any smoke with the locals, though he was also uncomfortable sitting by and watching something happen to his friend.

Shadow then spotted another one of his chums, Pain, who made hurried steps from the other side of the street toward the confrontation. Shadow knew Pain's temperament, so if he got out of the car with his mother's bullshit pistol and Pain saw it, that would only stoke the constantly burning fire in his friend's violent brain. No matter how it went down, however, Shadow would have his friend's back. He shoved his mother's gun in his pocket and parked the car.

Just as Shadow exited the Benz, the tension seemed to dissolve. Whatever Pain said to Malice must've given him some food for thought. Malice now turned his attention to Shadow and his silver Mercedes.

"All hail the prince of Five Points! What's good, Shadow?" Malice flashed a crocodile grin.

"Ain't shit," Shadow replied. "Just slid though the hood to check on my loved ones. We good out here?" He gave Pain a dap but stared straight at Malice.

"I think so. Are we good, Malice?" Fresh said with a smirk.

"Yeah, I guess you can breathe for now," Malice responded. "Yo, Shadow, what's up with your brother?"

"He's chilling."

"I bet," Malice said. "Dig, I've been trying to link with your brother for a minute. We got some things to discuss, but I feel like the nigga is avoiding me like I got the cooties."

Shadow shrugged. "Ghost moves how he moves. He's a busy guy."

"And I respect that, which is why I was thinking that maybe me and you can sit down? I run my angle down to you, and you can run it up the ladder."

"I don't get involved in that side of the family business." Shadow raised his hands and stepped back as if Malice had just tried to hand him a pistol in front of the police.

"Shorty, you talking to me like I'm out here wired for sound. It ain't even like that. You ain't gotta play the good-kid role with me. I know it's you who supplies these two knuckleheads with that bullshit cook-up they be out here trying to push. Next to the Clarks, the Kings are the best game in town and I'm just trying to get in where I fit in. I even come offering a gift, if you'll just hear me out. Feel me?"

"I feel you, Malice, but I can't help you," Shadow said.

"So, it's like that?"

"Afraid it can't be no other way. When I see my brother, I'll pass the word along that you're trying to sit with him. Whether the feeling is mutual or not will all depend on Ghost. I can't speak for him." Shadow turned to his friends. "Y'all ready to boogie?" He was anxious to get away from Malice.

Fresh jumped into the passenger seat of the Benz, while Pain got in the back.

"Y'all fellas be well," Shadow said to Malice and his crew, giving a mock salute as he got back in the driver's seat.

"I could tell you the same, King Shadow," Malice said. "It's spooky in the neighborhood lately. These young boys on some real hungry shit and not all of them care where the meal comes from."

"I grew up in a house full of predators," Shadow replied without giving Malice the respect of looking at him as he spoke. "I think I'll be okay." He turned the ignition and peeled off with his friends.

Once Shadow's Benz pulled away, one of Malice's henchmen came up behind him and put a hand on his shoulder. "Can't believe that pussy nigga was up on the ave trying to talk tough. He only popping shit because his brother is a shooter."

"Shadow ain't no tough guy, but he ain't no pussy," Malice said, watching the Benz turn the corner. "Quiet as he is, he's probably the more dangerous of the brothers because he's so damn sneaky. That kind of nigga can get you killed without ever having to touch a gun."

* * *

"Damn, it ain't even ten a.m. and y'all out here getting caught up in bullshit?" Shadow said to his friends as they pulled into traffic.

"It was *this* nigga who went and poked the bear." Pain gestured at Fresh.

"I ain't poke shit. I was checking that nigga about him being disrespectful. Let me tell you what he did."

After Fresh gave Shadow and Pain the short version of what had gone down earlier, the friends fumed in the car, throwing insults at Malice.

"That's some real sucker shit," Pain said. "I should've blown that nigga open." He rotated the razor over his tongue.

"And got your simple ass shot," Shadow said to him. "Homie was foul for talking that slick shit, and I'm glad Fresh called him on it. He stood up for himself. On the flip side, Malice is a killer. When you get into it with dudes like that, you need to be prepared to go all the way with it."

"And you saying I'm not willing?" Fresh said.

"If I didn't think you were willing if it came to that, I wouldn't keep company with you," Shadow answered. "All I'm saying is that with dudes like Malice you have to be careful. He's a petty, jealous-hearted nut. The type of dude who will catch you coming in the building on the late-night and pop you for some shit that might've happened between you two months prior. Dudes like him love to feel like they're making an example of somebody just for the clout."

"I hear you, Shadow," Fresh said. "I know what Malice is about, and I don't want no smoke with him, but I couldn't let that shit ride."

"So now what? Fresh is supposed to walk around on eggshells hoping that Malice ain't holding a grudge?" Pain asked from the backseat. Shadow knew he was looking for an excuse to get active.

Shadow thought on the question for a moment before answering, "Nah, not at all. That shit with Malice was light so it probably ain't gonna turn into nothing. But if you'd rather be safe than sorry, I can call my cousin Monster. Only thing about calling niggas like Monster is he ain't coming to trade threats. He's gonna push Malice's brain back. I don't give a fuck either way. What you trying to do, Fresh?"

Fresh thought about it. True, he was worried about what would happen between Malice and himself if they butted heads again and he wasn't under the protection of Shadow and Pain. Was it really over and done with, or was the gangster just rocking him to sleep? The latter was a strong possibility, but Fresh couldn't bring himself to cosign another man's death. He was a hustler, not a killer. He didn't want that stain on him. "Nah, man, I'm good," he finally said.

Pain sucked his teeth; he'd wanted Fresh to give Shadow the green light. He leaned forward, invading the space between the driver and passenger. "Do I get a vote?"

"No," Shadow told him. "If Fresh says it's over, we'll leave it at that."

Pain plopped back onto his seat, pouting like a child.

"But one day that muthafucka is gonna get what he deserves," Fresh said to himself more than anyone else.

"Well, obviously it ain't gonna be none of your doing. But since you ain't with the action, get with the drugs." Pain dug into his pants and pulled out a plastic bag of weed, which he tossed at Fresh. "Roll up."

"Laugh now, but we'll see how funny it is when he's in the dirt!" Fresh did hate Malice and longed for the day when he tried to bully someone who was willing to go the distance with him. He opened the bag of weed and was about to start breaking up buds when Shadow stopped him.

"Y'all must be crazy if you think we're gonna smoke in my mom's car. You can roll up in here, but we'll smoke at the spot."

CHAPTER 11

S hadow took the long way to their destination, cutting in and out of various blocks. He could've made a straight shot up Nostrand, but he wanted to be seen. He knew how gossip traveled, and he hoped all the local chickenheads and jealous niggas would spread the word that he was in the hood and riding as clean as the Board of Health.

Fresh and Pain traded jokes and war stories, as was their way when they all got together. Shadow only half listened. He was focused on the landscape. Between his mounting workload in school and his demanding family life, he found that his trips back to the block were becoming less and less frequent. In fact, had his mother not sent him on a mission that day, he probably wouldn't have come down here at all. He still had a bunch of paperwork to do for college. Between the FAFSA applications and working with his guidance counselors on financial aid applications, the process was kicking his ass. He knew that if his father wanted to, he could bankroll the tuition for any school Shadow wanted to go to, but Chance wanted him to experience the lumps and bumps of a regular high school senior. Further complicating things was the fact that his parents insisted he attend an HBCU, which not only limited his choices but the amount of aid he could get. The HBCUs were notoriously cheap when it came to academic scholarships.

All this thinking brought Shadow back to the task his mother had sent him on. "Yo, y'all seen Millie around lately?"

"Not in a few weeks, at least. Why, everything okay?" Pain knew Millie's backstory and how the family kept her at a distance. If they'd sent Shadow, of all people, to look for her, then maybe something was wrong.

"Everything's good," Shadow said. "My mom just wants her at her function tonight, though I don't know why."

"Maybe because she wants all her kids with her on her birthday?" Pain suggested. "Shadow, you know I know what time it is with your big sister. I see her out here lurking and shit. That girl is a whole trip with no luggage, but she's still your mama's baby. Ain't nothing short of her drowning a bag of kittens is gonna change that."

"I know, but I just don't understand her. Dawg, Millie could have anything she wanted if she just did right. There is nothing my parents wouldn't do for that girl."

"Who says she isn't getting everything she wants?" Pain said. "Respectfully, a friend's greatest joy is a blast. No amount of money or gifts you shower them with can even come close to the feeling of a good high. I ain't speaking on some hearsay shit, these are facts. Y'all know my story—both my parents and half my uncles were all out there on that shit at one time or another. You think they gave a shit about what they were doing to their families? Hell no, because an addict only cares about one thing! I understand better than most the sickness of addiction. Why do you think I don't do anything heavier than weed and maybe a little drink? My uncle is one of the strongest dudes I know, but that rock pushed him to sucking dick at bus stations to get that blast money right. Drugs can take you completely out of yourself."

Shadow stayed silent, reflecting on his friend's words. Pain wasn't the most educated man that Shadow kept company with, but he had a wisdom that couldn't be learned at any university.

He was a child of the streets and it showed in his walk, his talk, and, most importantly, the way he interpreted the world around him—a world increasingly alien to Shadow.

"So, what we gonna do? Ride around looking for Millie all day?" Fresh asked, hoping the answer would be no. After the morning he'd just had, the last thing he wanted to do was spend the rest of the day riding around looking for a crackhead.

"Nah," Shadow said. "I gotta catch up with her at some point today. I promised my mom as much. Right now, I'm just trying to get blazed."

"I second that motion!" Pain declared.

A few minutes later, they turned onto Jefferson Avenue, Shadow's old block. The parking gods were kind to them and they found a spot at the end of the street, near Marcus Garvey Boulevard.

As they walked to the apartment, Shadow was greeted every few feet by a new person. People clapped his shoulder and hollered at him from across the street, calling his name with reverence. He felt like the president. The residents of Jefferson Avenue loved the King family. Not just because they were hood royalty but also because Chance always made sure to take care of his own, even after he started making bank and moved off the block. Back when they still lived in Bed-Stuy, there was never a Christmas where a kid went without a toy or a Thanksgiving where a family didn't have a turkey.

Chance King was a good man, but that had nothing to do with the money he shelled out in the hood around the holidays. He understood that to be a great king, he had to be loved by his subjects. When the people where you did your dirt loved you, it granted you a sort of diplomatic immunity. The neighborhood turned a blind eye to Chance's dirt, lying to authorities for him when they had to. This allowed the Kings to run their criminal enterprise with impunity in those neighborhoods.

"I gotta hit the store," Fresh announced as they approached Shadow's building.

"What you need?" Pain asked, annoyed. He was ready to go upstairs and get blazed.

"They ain't got what I need at the bodega on Garvey," Fresh told him, heading to the next corner before anyone could protest.

"That joker," Shadow said, amused, taking a seat on the stoop in front of his family's building.

"Knowing him, he's probably going to the liquor store," Pain said, joining him on the stoop.

Shadow glanced at his watch. "It ain't even twelve o'clock yet."

"That's never stopped him before," Pain said, laughing. He pulled a cigar from his pocket and split it open, dumping the tobacco on the steps. As he began breaking weed into the empty husk, a dark thought crossed Shadow's mind.

"Say, what's up with that shit with Malice? You think something is going to come of it?"

Pain appeared to give the question some thought. "I don't think so. Malice was just showing out. He knows Fresh ain't no real threat. Besides, I hear he's got bigger problems to deal with. Rumor has it there's a crew from the East looking to expand. They've been playing Malice's territory real close and it's looking like they're gonna make a play."

"Malice has been running things on this side for years. Who would be dumb enough to try and rock that boat?" Shadow said.

"You remember that boy Cheese?"

Shadow searched his mental Rolodex, straining to put a face to the name. "I think so. The kid who Fresh used to hang with before he started running with us, right? He's a career soldier. I can't see him making a boss move."

"Not him, the kid who he's getting money with now," Pain told him. "They call him the Black Jew or some crazy shit like that. I hear he gets busy."

"I thought Malice had an army behind him." Shadow knew Malice more through reputation than anything else, but one thing he was certain of was that he was strong in Brooklyn.

"With everybody dying, going to jail, or getting out of the life, Malice's army has dwindled. That's probably why he keeps trying to plug in with Ghost. He needs the extra muscle to keep them young boys from overrunning him."

"I doubt that's going to happen," Shadow said.

"You know something I don't?"

"Maybe . . . Between you and me, I overheard Ghost talking about some shit, saying something about a fake Big Willie nigga on Nostrand who violated. I think it had something to do with his fiancée, Kelly. I didn't think about it before, but I'm willing to bet he was talking about Malice."

"Sounds about right. It wouldn't be the first time Malice tried to push up on somebody's broad and had to get checked. When he drinks, he'll put his dick in anything with a hole."

"If he was trying to push up on Kelly, the only hole in his future will be the one in his head," Shadow said.

"See, now this is all starting to make sense. I don't think it's a coincidence that Malice starts having trouble with these cats around the same time he disrespect's Ghost's lady. I love your brother like my own, but he's a sensitive nigga at heart. I can't see him letting something like that slide. Honestly, I wouldn't be surprised if it was Ghost who put the battery in those East New York cats to get at Malice."

Shadow hadn't considered this. Ghost was quick to violence, but war was something that he approached methodically. It was usually over money, blood, or respect. If he was behind it, then the latter had probably been the cause. It wouldn't be the first time Ghost had roped locals into doing dirt he didn't want blowing back on the family. He would pit one side against the other, and while they were distracted with shooting it out among each other, Ghost would blindside them with the killing blow. It was a tactic Chance had employed to establish a foothold in Brooklyn. By the time they saw him coming, he had already cemented himself.

A voice sounded from the doorway of the building. "C'mon, fellas. How many times do I have to ask you to stop using this stoop as a dumping ground?"

Shadow and Pain turned around to find a tall, well-built Black man with a neatly kept goatee and a red, black, and green kufi. He wore a hard scowl on his face, but it quickly softened when he recognized Shadow.

"Oh, hey there, Shadow," he said. "I didn't know that was you."

"What's going on, Mussa? Our fault about the blunt guts." Shadow got up and began sweeping the tobacco off the stairs and onto the street with his foot. Mussa was one of the few dudes who wasn't in the life that Shadow respected. But he hadn't always been a square. Once upon a time he had lived his life as a drug dealer and an addict. Things changed for the better when he found Islam in prison. Since then, he worked diligently to try to undo some of the harm he'd caused to his community when he ran the streets.

"It's all good, man," Mussa said. "You know I was once young and out there too, so I get it. I'm just trying to teach the young brothers and sisters the importance of maintaining where we lay our heads. Who is gonna give a damn about our hoods if we don't?"

"You're right about that," Shadow said. In his current

neighborhood, no trash littered the streets and there was no piss in the halls. The people in his area maintained their lawns and kept the streets in order. Shadow turned away from Mussa, but pivoted back around when he realized why he'd come to the neighborhood in the first place. "Say, have you seen my sister Millie around lately?"

"Not in a couple of days. I bumped into her the other night and let her borrow twenty dollars, but that was the last I saw of her."

Shadow shook his head. "Sorry about that, Mussa. I'll cover her debt." He reached into his pocket, but Mussa stopped him.

"Don't worry about it. I never expected Millie to pay me back. I understand how it is when you're out there. I tried to talk to her about getting clean, but—"

"She wasn't trying to hear it. That girl has been in and out of treatment for years and just can't seem to get her shit together. I don't know why my mom doesn't just lock her ass away somewhere and make her get clean!"

"That's not how this disease works, Shadow," Mussa explained. "An addict has to want to get clean. They have to hit their bottom, so to speak. Even then, sometimes it's not enough. Sobriety is a two-way street."

"What was your bottom?" Pain asked. "What made you decide to get clean?"

"I died," Mussa said. "I was maybe a year or so into my bid when it happened. Even in prison, I was still running around getting high and doing foul shit to people. Same as when I was on the street. Ran afoul of some dudes and to pay me back they made sure I got a hot-shot. The dose was meant to be lethal and it almost was. I had a massive heart attack and flatlined for about a minute and a half—or so I'm told. I guess Allah wasn't done with me yet. During my recovery, I met a good brother who worked as a prison orderly and he brought me into the Nation. I've been walking the righteous path ever since."

"That's some story, Mussa."

"It's my testimony. I was a hundred times worse of a fiend than your sister, Shadow. If I was able to get my shit together, there may still be hope for her too."

"I hope so," Shadow said, thinking of all the nights he listened to his mother sobbing behind her bedroom door over Millie.

"Allah doesn't make mistakes," Mussa said, placing a hand on Shadow's shoulder. "Not to change the subject, but I'm actually glad I bumped into you today, Shadow."

"What's up?"

"Well, the hot-water heater for the building is busted again. This is the third time in the last few months that it's gone out and we're getting tired of having to boil water so we can bathe our babies."

"Damn, that's messed up. Somebody's definitely gotta get that taken care of. It's just gonna keep getting colder out."

"And this is why I'm speaking to you about it. I've been on the building manager, but that fool acts like I'm speaking a foreign language. I know your dad still owns the building so I was hoping you could get in his ear and let him know what's going on."

"Maybe, but I don't know how much good it's gonna do. My dad is a busy guy with his campaign and all. Besides, he's overseeing the rehab projects. Even with the commercial properties, he only peeks in on them from time to time. Everything else he leaves to one of the Realtors that works for him. Maybe I can put you in touch with one of them?"

"I was kind of hoping that Chance would take a personal interest, since you guys did live here at one point."

"Mussa, I'm gonna keep it a buck with you, because I respect you. This building is the lowest on the ladder of my dad's properties. The dump barely brings in the money it takes to maintain it. The only reason he even bought it was to be a constant reminder of how fucked up our lives could've been. Real humbling shit." Shadow's response came out more cruel than he intended.

"So, since the Kings have moved on up, it's fuck the little man?" Mussa said.

"I feel your pain, Mussa, but you know how that shit goes, right?"

"Nah, Shadow, I don't. Tell your dad I said thanks for staying true to who he is," Mussa said, then stalked off down the block.

"What the fuck is his problem?" Shadow said.

"You don't get it, and I hope you never have to." Pain shook his head. Shadow was one of his best friends, but sometimes his lack of compassion for the less fortunate bothered him.

Before Shadow could ask Pain what he meant, Fresh came bouncing back around the corner. The plastic bag swinging in his hand said that Pain had been right about Fresh's destination. There was something about those black liquor store bags that stood out.

Shadow eyed the bag suspiciously. "Bruh, it's way too early for Henny or vodka, so I hope whatever you got in there is easy."

"Scary-ass nigga," Fresh teased. "I thought that in honor of us all getting together like old times, I'd go with a throwback." He pulled one of the two bottles from the bag and held it up proudly. It was a peach Cisco. "What y'all know about this?"

"I know the last time I drank one, I woke up in jail," Pain said, trotting up the stairs and into the building.

"Shadow?" Fresh held the bottle out to him.

"No thanks," Shadow said, following Pain into the building.

Fresh shrugged. "Fuck it. More for me." He twisted the cap off and took a deep swig before trailing his friends inside.

CHAPTER 12

"So, tell me why we're doing this again?" Monster said. He was again behind the wheel, but Ghost sat in the backseat, changing out of his suit into something better equipped for his next destination.

"Because an example needs to be set," Ghost repeated, having already gone over the plan with Monster several times. He slipped into a pair of gray sweatpants and pulled a matching hoodie over his head.

"Weren't you setting an example when you put these little off-brand niggas on the case?"

"And have they done what I asked?" Ghost answered. Monster was silent. "Exactly. When I ask a muthafucka to do something, I expect it to get done. Especially when they're being well compensated."

"I hear you, Ghost, but you gotta remember that these are kids you're dealing with. They're out here in the streets playing heavy, but they don't really know about war. You can't expect them to move how you move without having been properly trained."

"Were we properly trained the first time your dad put us out into the field?" Ghost asked. He didn't wait for his cousin to answer. "Hell no, Uncle Colt threw us into the deep end of the pool and dared us to drown. This ain't organized sports. We ain't got no coach. There's no participation trophy. This is the trap—we learn as we go. Some niggas is just remedial about the shit, so I'm just gonna give them a refresher course."

"You know you could've saved yourself the headache if you'd just let me and some of the guys come over here and get to it," Monster said. "That nigga would've been a stain by now."

"I know, Cousin. Everybody knows that you're my guy, so the effect would've been the same. I need to make this a local solution to a local problem, so that way when I make my play, the natives are on my side."

"I gotta admit, you're one wicked bastard, Ghost. You got a knack for turning people against each other in order to get what you want."

"It's all a part of the game, baby boy. If you ain't a part of the royal family then you're a tool to be used," Ghost replied.

"I'll keep that in mind," Monster said with a sly grin. He pushed the whip deeper into Brooklyn, where they were to rendezvous with the cats Ghost needed to see. Attempting to get around traffic, Monster jumped on Marcus Garvey Boulevard. As he passed through the neighborhood, he spotted a very familiar silver Mercedes. "Ain't that your mom's car?"

Ghost looked out the window and saw the Benz. It was indeed the same make and model but he highly doubted it was his mother's car. "Of all the places she could be spending the morning of her birthday, I doubt this shithole neighborhood is one of them."

"You're probably right," Monster said, giving the car one last curious glance.

Twelve minutes later they parked at their destination, a playground on Ralph Avenue. They were early, but the young man they were meeting was already there. His name was Judah, known in some circles as the Black Jew. According to lore, his family were direct descendants of Judah, the fourth son of Jacob. Monster suspected it was a rumor that Judah created to bolster his legend. Back when Monster first met the guy, he was a dusty little stickup kid trying to get his weight up. Now, dressed in a Gucci sweat suit and sitting on the hood of a white Lexus outside the playground entrance, he no longer resembled the dust ball he had been before Ghost started feeding him. Monster didn't dislike Judah, but he didn't trust him either. Judah almost reminded him of himself when he was on the come-up, and that wasn't a good thing.

In the months since Ghost started dealing with Judah, the guy was never on time for anything. Even his pickups and drops-offs were late. He was a kid who just didn't respect other people's time. That being said, seeing him show up early for the meeting with Ghost, especially in light of everything going on, gave Monster pause. "I don't like this," he muttered, quickly assessing the playground and surrounding area. Judah wasn't alone. Standing at his side was his pet pit bull, Cheese. Judah couldn't take a shit without Cheese being there, offering to wipe his ass. There was also a girl. She was cute—not pretty—with light skin and full hips. She leaned against Judah's car, twirling one of her long braids around her finger while scrolling through her phone. Across the street, a Honda sedan idled. Inside it were two dudes pretending not to be clocking Ghost and Monster. The whole situation felt off.

"You don't like nothing as far as Judah is concerned," Ghost said before stepping out of the car. Monster mumbled something inaudible as he opened the door.

At the sight of Ghost approaching, Judah pushed himself off the hood of his vehicle and moved to greet him. "What's good, big homie?" he said as they dapped.

"I was hoping that you could tell me," Ghost started, "why that piece of business I put you on ain't been taken care of yet."

Judah looked at the hard-faced man watching his back, then turned to Ghost. "We on it, man. It's just taking us a little longer than anticipated. This dude isn't exactly a pushover."

"I'm aware of this, which is why I thought I was putting one of my most qualified young boys on the job. Maybe I was wrong in that assessment of you, J?"

Judah's jaw tightened. He glanced over at the girl, who had stopped scrolling through her phone and was now paying attention to the conversation. "Chelsea, take a quick walk to the store and get me a water."

Chelsea sucked her teeth, but didn't argue, and stomped off in the direction of the store. When she was gone, Judah addressed Ghost.

"Ghost, I respect you, but we need to be clear on something: I get busy in these streets, fam. I don't give a fuck who it is or how strong—if they're in the way of progress then they go. That's on my kids. Now, I get it. Malice has pissed in your Cheerios, but you need to understand something. This ain't some sucka-ass nigga trying to make a name for himself. Malice has been in position for years. He's strong out here, so I need to move right on this so I can get close enough to him to do what you're asking of me. This ain't some random nigga who I can just pay off his bitch to leave the door unlocked so my boys can do him dirty."

This last line stung. Judah was referring to a rumor circulating about how Ghost managed to acquire a piece of contested territory in South Jamaica, Queens, held by a vicious gangster named Black Tone. Usually when the King family applied pressure, people folded without putting up much of a fight, but not Black Tone. He was willing to take Ghost to war for what was his. Tone was a savage and had a nice-sized crew behind him, so taking the territory by force was easier said than done. This was when Ghost got crafty with it. Instead of going at Black Tone head up like a real solider, Ghost paid off Tone's girl to double-cross him. One night, while Tone slept over at her house, she neglected to lock the front door. Ghost slipped in and blew the sleeping man's head off, then killed his girl. Whether this rumor was true or not could never be confirmed, since Ghost was the only one alive who knew what had happened. All the streets knew was that when Ghost planted the King flag in South Jamaica, there was no one to contest him.

"If I were you, I'd watch my mouth," Monster warned Judah now.

Judah raised his hands in surrender. "My fault."

"Bottom line, you gonna push this nigga off the planet or do I need to reach out to someone else to give that turf to?" Ghost asked.

"You know I want that hood, big homie. I'm gonna get this done. I'm just trying to move correct. I gotta wait until I catch him slipping, because my team ain't deep enough for a straight-up war. I'd like to keep my casualties to a minimum."

"If you need some extra muscle, I got no problem having Monster or some of the other guys come through and help you out," Ghost said. "The only thing about that is that you'd have to break bread with them on the spoils, and we all know how greedy my cousin can be." He nodded in Monster's direction.

"I could go for a slice of that pie," Monster said, licking his big lips. It was a bluff, he and Ghost both knew it, but Judah didn't.

"Nah, we'll take care of it," Judah responded.

"That's the go-getter attitude that made me recruit you in the beginning," Ghost said, adjusting the lapel of Judah's sweat suit jacket. "Change is coming. I'll need people around me who I know can get shit done. Make this happen and I'll make you the lord of all that you survey."

"I got you, Ghost," Judah vowed.

After a few last words, it was time to part company. Ghost had tested Judah, pushing his buttons to see what kind of reaction he would get from the young hustler. If he had bucked against him, Ghost would've known he wasn't right for the position Ghost planned to put him in. But Judah handled himself well, which was a good thing. He probably thought Ghost was tight about him not taking care of Malice, but Ghost was hardly as upset as he pretended to be. It was all part of the test. Be it by Judah's hand or someone else's, Malice was dead and his neighborhood would soon come under the Kings' rule. In truth, the few strips that Malice controlled weren't even worth the effort. It was the principal of what he had done that required Ghost to make an example of him.

"I can't believe we going to war with them old niggas from the Stuy over a bitch," Cheese mumbled under his breath. Judah shot him a look.

"What did you just say?" Ghost said, turning to him.

And there it was, the elephant in the room. Ghost had been aware of Malice and his operation for years, but until recently the man hadn't really been of much concern. That changed when Malice and Ghost's fiancée ended up at the same party. Ghost was away on business and Kelly was having a girls' night out. According to people who witnessed what happened, Malice was drunk and trying to hit on everything in a skirt, including Kelly. When she blew him off, he took it personal and palmed her ass in front of everyone at the party. She tried to swing on him, but luckily some guys loyal to the King family stopped anything from going down. It wasn't that serious. In fact, Kelly had never bothered mentioning it to Ghost. Someone else had. Ghost could've let it go, but he had a reputation to protect. A man who laid hands on his girl was a man not long for life. He could've simply killed Malice, but death wasn't enough. He wanted to break him before he sent him on a one-way trip to the spirit world. This was why he had recruited Judah.

All eyes were now on Cheese. He knew he had fucked up by speaking out of turn, but it was out there. He wanted to swallow his tongue, though he couldn't run the risk of looking like a sucker in front of Judah. "No disrespect to you, Ghost. I'm just saying that there is a lot of blood about to be spilled because Malice pushed up on a broad you're fucking."

"So that's what you think this is about? Some random piece of pussy?" Ghost asked in an icy tone.

"I figured the pussy must've been fire if you're willing to go to war over it." Cheese meant it as a joke, but the humor was lost on Ghost.

"Say, Cuz," Ghost called over his shoulder to Monster, "remember that mess I said we were gonna make?"

"Say less." Monster stalked forward.

Judah stepped between Monster and Cheese. "Chill out, fellas."

"Move or bleed, lil' nigga," Monster said, shoving Judah to the side as if he were little more than a curtain blocking a doorway. By the time he got to Cheese, the guy was reaching for something in his pants, but it never made it out.

Monster slapped Cheese with so much force that the dudes in the car across the street heard his jaw break. They fumbled out of the car and rushed over to where the fight was happening, only to be met by Ghost and his two 9mms.

"Fuck is y'all lil' niggas about to do?" Ghost challenged, leveling his guns at their heads.

"Ghost, this ain't necessary!" Judah said, watching as Monster mercilessly throttled Cheese.

"Oh, but I think it is," Ghost said without turning around.

"See, when I speak softly, y'all act like y'all don't hear me, so now I gotta raise my voice."

Monster punched, kicked, and stomped Cheese like he had just caught the man fondling his little sister. There was blood everywhere. When his arms finally tired, Monster reached into his jacket and produced a snub-nosed revolver. He roughly jammed it between Cheese's split lips. "Sleepy time, shorty."

"That's enough," Ghost told him.

"Fuck you mean? When we go, we go all the way!" Monster snarled over his shoulder. All day he had itched for some action, and now Ghost was trying to deny him his glory. He wasn't feeling it.

"I think Cheese has received my message. Ain't that right, Cheese?" Ghost asked, but Cheese was unconscious.

Reluctantly, Monster withdrew the gun from the guy's mouth, but not before hitting him in the face with the butt for good measure.

"You ain't have to do all that, Ghost," Judah said, barely able to control his anger. "Cheese got a big month, but he's one of mine. If he was wrong then it was my place to chastise him, not yours."

Ghost shrugged. "No need to thank me for doing you a favor. I like you, Judah. You're gonna be a star out here one day if you can just learn to get out of your feelings. I told you when we struck our little bargain that you're in the deep end now. You're gonna either swim or drown. Your choice."

As Ghost walked back to the car, Monster lingered, watching Ghost's back just in case somebody tried to retaliate for what had just gone down. Ghost strode along as if he didn't have a care in the world. If he had bothered to turn around, he would have seen the look of death Judah shot him.

* * *

"That wasn't smart, Ghost," Monster said once they were back in traffic and far from the playground.

"Cheese was out of line."

"That we can agree on, but pouncing on one of the niggas who you've just allied with to pull off a hostile takeover is sending mixed signals. In one breath you say you're gonna feed these dudes and in the next you order me to beat the shit out of one of their own. How you think it's gonna look on Judah if he lets this go? He'll lose the respect of his soldiers."

"Then I'll provide him with a new army," Ghost said. "What? You feeling some type of way that I had you put hands on that nigga?"

"Not at all. I couldn't give a fuck about Cheese or Judah. We got an agreement with them young boys and the minute you put me on Cheese, you poisoned that deal. If you were gonna do it like that then we should've killed Cheese, Judah, and the rest of them, then started over. This could turn into a problem down the line."

Ghost knew that Monster was right. He had just acted off emotions and dressed it up as principle. As a result, he might have seriously damaged his relationship with Judah. Not that the partnership would make or break Ghost one way or the other, but he had gone too far to turn back. He was already committed to the takeover and would need to follow through. "I'll make this right with Judah," Ghost said. It was the closest he could go to issuing an apology.

Monster let it die after that. He doubted that Ghost even realized the extent of the insult levied against young Judah. That's because he could no longer recognize the signs. The same couldn't be said for Monster. His street senses hadn't been dulled by the finer things in life. He was a predator and could spot one of his own. And one thing was for certain—Judah was going to turn into a problem that would need solving. Monster planned to do just that.

CHAPTER 13

B y the time afternoon came, Chance was worn out. He had been out and about all day, making sure that all his ducks were in a row. He and Maureen had spent the last few weeks going over his battle plan, checking and double-checking to make sure that nothing had been missed. She still wasn't keen on the idea of him going all in with his political career, but she put her personal feelings to the side and stood with him as a true queen should. The process had been rough on her, which was all the more reason Chance wanted to make sure her birthday was one befitting a queen. Once he was done with his rounds, he was going to go home and make the rest of the night all about her.

The last stop Chance had to make before leaving the city was one that hadn't been on the schedule. Yet when Rocco Salvatore called and asked for a sit-down, it wasn't a request he could ignore. Any other time, Chance would've taken the summons as a slight, but these were delicate times and he knew he was treading in dangerous waters. He swallowed a bit of pride and decided to answer the summons for the sake of keeping the peace. He didn't fear Rocco like some of the other lords did, but he also knew better than to unnecessarily offend him. While Chance may have worn the crown of Five Points, Rocco was the tip of the spear. He sat at the head of one of the biggest Mafia families in the city. At full strength, he commanded at least one hundred hired guns, and so as long as Rocco was happy, those guns would all be at Chance's disposal.

When Stevie pulled up to the block, the first thing he noticed were two men lingering near the entrance of Rocco's building. Another man sat lookout in the window of a third-floor apartment in the building across the street. He was trying to be inconspicuous behind the laced curtain that covered the window, but Stevie's eyes were trained to pick out threats wherever they hid. "This shit smells funky to me, Chance," he muttered.

"That's the fish market on Williams Street you're smelling," Chance joked. He too shared his friend's uneasiness, but there was no sense in making an already tense situation worse. It was best to play it cool. "I should be back in about ten minutes." He reached for the door, but Chippie stopped him.

"If you're not, me and Stevie are coming in after you," she said.

Chance smiled and patted her hand. "That's good to know, darling, but I think I'll be okay."

Chance slipped from the car and made his way toward Rocco's current residence, an apartment building that had been there longer than either of them. Until several years ago, the mobster had lived in a modest house out in Queens with his wife and three kids. Has wife had passed two years back and both his daughters moved away, leaving only Rocco and his son Dickey in New York. And Dickey was a straight-up soldier. With all that he had sought to protect by moving to Queens now gone, Rocco decided it was time to get back in the thick of things. He wanted to live out the twilight of his life in the same neighborhood he had grown up in, in the apartment where his dad kicked the shit out of him and his siblings. The only difference now was that Rocco owned the building, and he was no longer the kicked; he was the kicker.

The place sat just above a Chinese bakery, so the building and all the apartments always smelled like fresh pastries. The two men guarding the outside of the building nodded in greeting to the king of Five Points. They moved aside and allowed him to enter without patting him down. (Something only known to a select few was that when Rocco purchased this building, he evicted all the tenants and installed his most trusted capos and killers in the apartments. You'd have a better chance of getting next to the president than you would Rocco.)

Chance took his time walking up the three flights of stairs that led to Rocco's apartment. When he stepped onto the third floor, he immediately smelled weed, which was odd because Rocco didn't allow drugs in his presence, especially where he laid his head. It didn't take long to identify the source of the smell. A card table was set up beyond the landing. A few of the younger mafiosi lounged around playing poker; Chance recognized one of them. He was young—not as old as Ghost but older than Shadow. His black hair was tapered on the sides. A red sweat suit two sizes too big hung on his lanky frame. Around his neck lay a gold chain with a large medallion depicting St. Nicholas, the patron saint of thieves. The young mafiosi stood as a sign of respect, all except the man with the chain, who glared at Chance.

"*It Ain't the Boot Who Sat by the Door*," the man said. "Ain't that what the book was called?"

"You and I both know that isn't the title, Dickey," Chance replied, "just like we know I don't tolerate disrespect. Not even from Rocco's kid."

Dickey let his scowl slip into a smile. "I was only busting your balls, Chance. I meant no disrespect."

"Sometimes I wonder," Chance said. "I gotta say, I'm surprised to see you here. Last I heard, that temper of yours had landed you in some trouble. Attempted murder, wasn't it?"

"It's more of a he said, she said. Only *she* never showed up in court to say anything. You ain't the only one who knows Jews in high places," Dickey boasted.

Something about this last comment didn't sit well with Chance. He kept that to himself and tried to stick to business. "I'm here to speak with your father."

"He told me you got some things to whisper about. Face-to-face conversations are big-boy talk. I guess I gotta wait until I'm officially sitting at the table before I can tap in on those."

"What's for us is for us and what ain't, ain't," Chance said. When he stepped around the table to get to Rocco's apartment, Dickey rose to block his path.

"I'll need to pat you down," Dickey informed him.

"You can't be serious." Ever since Chance's first time visiting Rocco in this building, he had never been subjected to a search.

"There's a war going on outside that no man is safe from," Dickey said, referencing the lyrics to a Mobb Deep song. "Bad things happening to good people, so I'm just trying to make sure my pops is good. You understand, don't you?" He took a step in Chance's direction, but the king moved out of his reach.

"The only thing I understand is if you put your dick-beaters on me, we're gonna have a problem," Chance said. This had nothing to do with security; this was Dickey attempting to disrespect Chance and expecting him to sit for it, which he wouldn't.

The other mafiosi now circled him. Each of them knew that Dickey was playing at some bullshit, but he was also their boss so there wasn't much they could do except fall in line. Chance was unbothered. Though Dickey was a dangerous young man, without his father's backing he wasn't anywhere near the level of Chance. He was a baby stumbling around the house in his father's shoes, and sometimes he had to be reminded of that.

A wall of tension built between the men as they eyed each other. Dickey had never cared for the Kings because he believed that when the monarchy of Five Points was established, it should've been a Salvatore wearing the crown, not a King. The Salvatores had history and pedigree, but it was the Kings who had the plan. Even Dickey's father had stood with Chance on this because he understood the long game. Crowning Chancellor King the king of Five Points was a business decision, not a personal one. Unfortunately, Dickey Salvatore had never managed to see it that way, nor was he very good at hiding his feelings.

"You two done jerking each other off?" a voice called out, cutting through the tension. At the end of the hall, standing in the doorway of Rocco's apartment, was Vincent Apora. In his prime, Vincent had been the Salvatore family's high executioner, but two heart attacks and Father Time had relegated him to a sort of personal assistant for Rocco. He didn't get his hands dirty much because of his age and condition, but you'd be a fool to think Vincent wasn't still dangerous. Everybody respected the old-timers, even the young mafiosi.

"Give me a break, Vinnie," Dickey said, taking a step back. "I was just having a little fun with the king."

"If you invested as much energy into the business as you did fucking off and looking for a good time, your dad would've been able to officially retire by now," Vincent spat. He motioned for Chance to join him.

With a smile on his face, Chance bumped past Dickey and moved into the apartment. Vincent hesitated for a moment to give Dickey and his crew warning looks before stepping into the apartment and slamming the door.

"I'm sorry about that, Chance," Vincent said, locking the door behind them once they were both inside.

Chance patted him on the shoulder. "No need to apologize, Vinnie. I know better than most the ignorance of youth." Lowering his voice, he continued, "I have to say that this sit-down was unexpected. Anything I need to be concerned about?" Chance and Vincent went back even further than he and Rocco. They had run in the same circles as kids and broken some of the same laws.

"All I can tell you is that you weren't called here to die," Vincent told him. "Anything besides that is between you and Rocco." This answer did little to reassure Chance.

They found Rocco in the living room, hunched over a chessboard. Thick cigar smoke wafted from the burning stogie in the ashtray, crowning his white head. He must've sensed Chance's presence because he raised a finger, motioning for the king to give him a minute. His meaty hand touched the tip of the black bishop, but then he paused. After a moment, he decided to move his knight instead. He sat back to admire his work before turning his attention to his visitor.

"You still play, Chance?" Rocco asked in a voice that had grown harsh from decades of smoking. He motioned for Chance to take a seat across from him.

"Every day in the streets, but not so much on the board anymore," Chance replied, sitting down in the wooden chair.

"Shame, because you were pretty good."

Chance picked up the white king and studied it. "I had an amazing teacher." He had long understood the basics of the game, but it was Rocco who'd taught him how to really play. They used to sit in front of his house in Queens for hours, drinking red wine and playing chess. But those days were over; they were different men now. After a moment of silence, Chance asked, "So, why the summons?"

"You of all people should know that I don't trust telephones."

"Must be something heavy if you needed to speak to me face-to-face."

"The weight of this conversation will depend on you," Rocco said, looking at Chance with menacing blue eyes. Those eyes were once so full of life, but now all they held was death.

"I'm afraid I don't understand, Rocco."

"Then let me clarify." Rocco folded his thick hands on the chessboard. "Some of our friends are concerned about this move you're about to make."

"C'mon, Rocco, it isn't like I just sprang this on you. You guys have all known for months. Having me 100 percent vested in politics and away from the bullshit completely can only be good for the monarchy."

Rocco shrugged his broad shoulders. "Maybe, maybe not. See, having one of our own rubbing elbows with politicians means that we all share in the perks that come with it. Once you leave the table, who is to say that you won't take your politician friends with you? After all, if you are no longer a part of the monarchy, then you'll have no obligation to it."

And there it was. Rocco had called Chance in not for himself, but to address the concerns of some of the other lords. This made Chance angry. Even before the monarchy, he had never been the puppet at the end of any puppeteer's strings.

"Respectfully, I started the monarchy. It was my plan and my influence that brought it together."

"Right on both counts. You were the man with the plan and the connections that brought everyone to the table, but it was the lords of the monarchy who made sure everyone stayed there," Rocco said. "Chance, I know your heart. You've always been a good and fair king, which is why I've never had a problem with you sitting at the head of the table. If you recall, I was one of your most passionate supporters and the one who personally placed that crown on your head. Now, some of my boys weren't happy with it, but it was what it was. I left you to the headaches that came with the crown and was content to sit back and reap the benefits."

"And that will continue, even when I'm gone. Ghost ascends to the throne."

"I love Ghost, but I think he's better suited as a general, not a king. There are some who fear his temper will lead the monarchy to ruin. Aside from that, Ghost doesn't have your reach. He hasn't cultivated the relationships that you have over the years."

"I can walk him through it until he's ready to lead on his own," Chance said.

"That arrangement would be fine by me, but unfortunately there are others who aren't as keen on such a plan. People are talking, Chance."

"And what are they saying, Rocco?"

"That maybe this was all part of your plan—to have your cake and eat it too, if you will. You still get to tap the resources of the monarchy through your proxy, but get to denounce us if things take a bad turn."

"And what do you believe?"

Rocco thought on the question before answering. "I believe that you are a man who sees something he wants and goes after it. The only problem is when you're so locked in on what's in front of you, sometimes you miss what's at your back."

"And what's that supposed to mean?"

"Relax, Chancellor. I'm not your enemy. In fact, you may find that I'm one of the few friends you have left when it's all said and done. Old friends, that is. As far as I'm told, you're making quite a few new ones."

Chance was caught off guard by this statement. Rocco must

have known about his meeting with Paul Schulman. Although he had suspected as much from Dickey's smart comment in the hallway, this was still cause for concern. If Rocco knew about the meeting, did he also know about the nature of it? What Chance and Paul had agreed to wouldn't hurt Rocco directly, but the fallout would be felt by the whole monarchy. Chance opened his mouth, ready to spin a tale for Rocco, but the mobster waved him silent.

"Chance, before you say something that changes how I feel about you, let me say this: I don't care who you do business with or what gods they worship. So long as your backdoor deals don't affect the bottom line of my family and the monarchy continues to thrive, it makes no difference to me. I can't say the same for some of our other constituents. The moves that you think you're making quietly are being heard, and sometimes when a message is received through a third party, it can be misconstrued by the recipients of these messages. Things can sometimes look like what they might not be."

"What is it that you're trying to say here?" Chance asked.

Rocco looked around him, a suspicious glint in his eye. It was only the two of them in the room, but you could never be sure who was listening. Rocco was paranoid like that, which was how he had managed to avoid growing old in prison like some of his associates. "I got love for you, Chance. You've always done right by me, so I'm telling you this as a friend and I should hope that what I'm about to say never leaves this room."

Chance nodded.

"You aren't the only one who the winds will be blowing for when you make this move. Some people are not fond of change. You're looking out for your own best interests, so you can't fault others for wanting to do the same."

"Somebody planning to move against me?" Chance asked.

"Nobody is stupid enough to move against you, so long as I call you my friend."

"And so if I shift to politics, we'll no longer be friends?"

"Chancellor, our relationship has always been built on who you are, not the imaginary crown you wear," Rocco said with a half smile. "Unfortunately, I'm getting on in years. I'm not long for this game or this world. I'm the head of this family, but in my old age, my words don't carry the same weight they once did. This has become a young man's game and we old-timers are only as valuable as what we bring to the table." He reached across the table and moved the black rook to take the white bishop, putting the black king into checkmate. "Once we have nothing more for the table, it has nothing more for us." He tipped over the black king on the chessboard.

Chance peered at the toppled piece. The old man's warning was clear. Chance had never expected the transition away from the streets to be an easy one. He was in too deep and too much hinged on him maintaining his seat at the table. Part of him wanted to call it off and continue to dance between both worlds, but he had come too far to turn back. The higher up he moved in government, the more thoroughly he'd be vetted, which could not only bring him down but the entire monarchy as well. Making a clean break would be best for all, especially his family. He was doing all of this to protect everyone. The monarchy may not have seen it now, but in time they would. In the event that they didn't, Chance would have to execute his contingency plan, and God be with whoever fell at the wrong end of that sword.

"As always, I appreciate your counsel, Rocco," Chance said. "I've got a few things that I need to take care of before I get ready for tonight. Will I be seeing you later at the dinner?"

"Sadly, this is a meal I'll have to miss. My gout has been giving me trouble." Rocco pointed to an ice pack wrapped around his foot that Chance hadn't noticed. "You understand, don't you?"

"Unfortunately, I understand all too well," Chance said with a heavy voice. "Thank you for being such a good friend to me over the years." He kissed the old man on both cheeks and made his exit.

CHAPTER 14

S hadow sat on the living room couch of his old apartment, as high as a jaybird. Pain had rolled up three bombers of some shit he had scored in Washington Heights. It smelled like cow dung when he lit it, but it was some of the most potent weed Shadow had ever smoked. He made a mental note to have Pain show him where he copped it so he could grab some for his school friends. Those white boys wouldn't be ready for that Heights fire!

Being back in his old apartment always felt weird. He could remember living there, but since his family moved out, the specific memories had started to fade. Even when he made these occasional visits, he felt out of place. It was small and cramped. Although there were three bedrooms, it hardly seemed big enough to accommodate his parents and siblings. The walls were a drab eggshell color and the ceiling was white stucco. The old gray carpet that once lined every inch of the house had been stripped to the bare brown baseboards. The floor tiles looked like they were coming up in some places, but no one cared enough to have someone come in and lay the tiles back down properly. After all, the apartment had become more of a symbol than a domicile.

Fresh slumped on a beanbag chair next to the window, sweating like a runaway slave. He had chugged one whole bottle of Cisco and made it halfway through the second before it all started kicking in. He'd spent a half hour in the bathroom, where Shadow assumed he was throwing up, before staggering out into the living room and collapsing onto the beanbag.

Though Pain was trying to pretend that he was good, Shadow could tell that he was feeling it too. For all the shit Pain talked about not rocking with the Cisco, Fresh convinced his ass to have a small cup of it. Pain could smoke with the best of them, but he had a very low tolerance for alcohol. He sat at the kitchen table trying to juggle two kitchen knives, almost cutting himself twice. Shadow wanted to tell him to chill out before he hurt himself, but there was something about the juggling that made him giggle, so he kept watching.

Suddenly, the doorknob rattled and Shadow shot up from his slump. The sound of a key sliding into the lock made Shadow blink in slow realization. Very few people had keys to this apartment. His parents wouldn't be caught dead back in the neighborhood and Ghost never came by. Not even the building manager had a key, or at least he wasn't supposed to. What if he'd gone behind the Kings' backs and made one?

Before Shadow could shake the fog of his inebriation, Pain was at the front door, knives in hands. Shadow eventually pulled himself to his feet and joined his friend. Pain was crouched military style, waiting to pounce on the intruder. Shadow opened his mouth to say something, but Pain raised his hand and silenced him. He was in combat mode and the best thing Shadow could do was to stay out of the way. Shadow's heart raced as the door creaked open and a man he didn't recognize stepped in. He was a rough-looking cat who wore his pants hanging off his ass and an oversized hoodie. Clutched in his arm was a brown paper bag. He was speaking to someone else bringing up his rear. Shadow's palms pooled with sweat as he waited for Pain to give the signal to strike. Once the man was fully inside the apartment, Pain made his move; with a fluid speed he pounced, catching the intruder by surprise. Pain hit him with a right cross, causing him to drop his paper bag and shatter whatever was inside it. Pain pinned the intruder to the wall, placing the knife against his throat. Shadow was about to move in on the second figure that had stepped into the apartment when he heard a familiar voice.

"What the fuck are you doing?" Millie said, looking back and forth between Pain and her shocked little brother.

Shadow found himself momentarily speechless. It had been awhile since he had seen Millie and she had lost a considerable amount of weight, so much so that the skinny jeans she wore looked baggy. There was a hungry look in her eyes and her once thick, rich hair was now thin and brittle. Shadow's heart broke seeing one of the two proud queens his mother raised reduced to such a state.

"That's a question I should ask you," Shadow said when he finally found his voice. "How did you get a key to the apartment?"

"Our mother gave me the key in case of an emergency, in case I ever found myself in need of a place to lay my head," Millie said.

"Lay *our* head, huh?" Shadow cut his eyes at the man Pain held against the wall. "That include bringing random hypes up in here?"

"Man, I ain't no hype!" the man protested. "Millie, who is these little niggas? Tell them to turn me loose!"

"They ain't nobody, Milton," Millie said. "Turn him loose, Pain."

Pain continued to hold the man, casting a worried glance at Shadow.

"Percy," Millie said, calling Pain by his given name, "why are you looking at my brother when I'm the one talking to you?" She used to babysit Pain when his mother went missing for days at a time, so she expected her word to carry weight. She folded her arms and waited. It wasn't until Shadow gave him the nod that Pain released the man named Milton. "Ain't this a bitch?" Millie went on, grinning. "I used to wipe your ass and now you acting like I'm some stranger. Since when did I have to start asking you to do things twice?"

"It ain't personal, Millie," Pain told her. He lowered his eyes when he passed her.

"I guess Daddy and Ghost ain't the only ones with a set of flunkies," Millie said with a snort. "What you doing here with these lowlifes anyhow? Why's your ass not in school?"

"Mama sent me to holla at you. It's a family matter." Shadow glanced at Milton, who stared sadly at the two broken forty-ounce bottles now shattered and puddled on the floor.

"I was about to go take care of something. Can it wait?" Millie asked. She'd yet to have her wake-up hit, and her insides were starting to twist in on themselves.

"No," Shadow said flatly. He knew exactly what was going on with her. It hurt him to see her in this condition, but instead of showing compassion he showed cruelty.

Millie knew that Shadow wasn't going to let it go and she didn't feel like fighting with him. The quicker she heard him out the quicker she could be rid of him and get back to the business of her wake-up fix. "Milton, sweetie, give me a sec to take care of this. I'll meet you in front of your building in like ten minutes."

"You must think I'm stupid," Milton responded. "You already spent my money to buy your blast. I take my eyes off you and you're probably going to give me the slip before I can get what's owed."

"Why don't you relax, homie?" Shadow said. "As soon as I'm done talking to my sister you can link back up and smoke as much crack as you want."

"Shorty, you need to watch where you casting them stones," Milton countered. "I don't smoke crack, but I did pay to get my dick sucked."

"What?" Shadow blurted out before swinging on Milton. Much to his surprise, his sister's companion fought back. Milton managed to land a nice blow on Shadow's chin, forcing him to stagger backward. Without thinking, Shadow pulled his mother's gun from his pocket and aimed it at the guy. "I should blow your fucking brains out for putting your hands on me!"

"Shadow, chill the fuck out," Pain said from behind him. "You shoot this nigga and you're gonna put your whole family at risk."

Shadow glared at Milton for a few ticks longer. Enraged that an inferior human had dared to put his hands on him in front of his friends and sister, Shadow didn't want to let this go. His pride was more wounded than his chin, and he felt his finger tightening on the trigger. All it would take was a split second and Milton would be out of there—but so would Shadow; there was no way he'd get away with it. Finally, he lowered the gun. "You're right." He handed the derringer to Pain. "But he still gotta get *this* work." Shadow pulled his new brass knuckles from his pocket and slipped them over his fingers.

He pummeled Milton, tearing into him with a ferocity that Pain hadn't really seen before. Milton screamed so loud that he spooked Fresh's drunk ass from his slumber. Every time Shadow hit the poor guy, you could hear something break. Pain had gone to battle against dudes with Shadow at his side before, so he knew that the prince could get busy, but that was only when forced. This was something different—it almost felt like a hate crime. Clearly, Shadow was getting something off his chest, and Pain intended to let him.

Pain eventually intervened when it seemed like Shadow

had shed whatever shit he was dealing with. Milton was barely conscious; a cluster of knots crowned his head. Pain and Fresh scooped the beaten man up and carried him out of the apartment. They decided to go out the back of the building and dump him on the next block for someone else to find.

While they were gone, Millie addressed Shadow: "You know, the older you get the more like the rest of them you become." She stared at the blood on the walls and floors. She was disappointed. How could she not be? Shadow was the sweet one of the family.

"At least I'm out here carrying myself like a King and not some two-bit junkie whore," Shadow said, inspecting his fist.

"Watch your mouth, little prince. You ain't too big to not still catch these hands." Millie raised her fists menacingly. She was a fighter, always had been. Growing up, she had even given Ghost a run for his money whenever they got into it. "Anyway, what did Mama send you to talk to me about?"

"Her birthday. She wanted me to see if you were going to make it to her party."

"Shit, her birthday ain't until April."

"What month do you think we're in?"

Millie searched her scattered brain, trying to piece together the date. "Damn," she said, realizing that she had no idea. "I'll, umm . . . I'll find the time to get her something and drop it off."

"What she wants more than anything is for you to be there tonight. We're having a big party in the city. We're celebrating Mama's birthday and announcing that Daddy's running for higher office. A lot of important people are going to be there, including some of Daddy's street business partners."

"I think I remember Lolli telling me something about it the last time we talked," Millie said.

"You keep in contact with Lolli?" Lolli had never mentioned this to Shadow.

"Besides Mommy, Lolli is the only one of you who don't treat me like Pookie from *New Jack City.*"

"Is that how you think the rest of us look at you?"

"Like you said, I'm moving like a *junkie whore* instead of a King," Millie spat. "It's cool though, I'm comfortable in my skin. How about the rest of you?"

"Meaning?"

"Meaning all of you live in the shadow of what the king and queen expect of you. Under that monarchy, your lives will never be your own. Me? I'm out here free, baby brother." Millie spread her arms for emphasis.

"How you screaming you're free when you're a slave to your addiction?"

"That's where you've got it wrong, little prince. I'm not a slave to cocaine, it's a slave to me. I knew from the first time I took a hit that this white bitch don't love me. For sure she makes me feel groovy, but those are only moments. For as long as I feed that bitch, she'll eat from my hand. The minute I can put oil in that burner, she'll leave me. I understand that this is the nature of our relationship so my expectations are never high."

"You've got a real fucked-up way of looking at things, Millie."

"An aftereffect of growing up as one of the King kids."

"Growing up a King is the best life anybody could ask for."

"Until it isn't," Millie said. "Shadow, things are good for you as long as they fall in line with what Mommy and Daddy want. God forbid you have an original thought. That's when they'll brand your ass an enemy of the monarchy."

"You're exaggerating."

"Am I? By the time you and Lolli were born, Chance and

Mom were a little older and finally grew consciences about the way they lived and the things they dragged their kids through. Everyone in Chancellor and Maureen King's lives was a chess piece, including us. You don't believe me? Ask Ghost about his first failed engagement."

"The only person Ghost has ever been engaged to is Kelly," Shadow said.

Millie gave a throaty laugh. "The fact that you're ignorant to one of the most historical blunders in our family history tells me that you're walking around with blinders on. You may want to pull them off on your own before someone else snatches them off. You want a history lesson, ask Uncle Chapman about it. He's a useless piece of shit, but you won't find a better source of gossip than him. What I'll tell you about the incident is that once I saw what your father tried to do to his favorite son, I realized that we were all expendable if it suited the needs of the king. That was around the time when I decided that before I allowed myself to be a pawn on someone else's chessboard, I'd be a queen on my own."

"And this is your queendom?" Shadow glanced around the apartment.

"Touché, little brother. Nah, man. This is a temporary setback. If you'd been through some of the shit I've been through trying to be a proper princess, you might've turned to drugs to numb your pain too. As King kids, we're all one push away from either becoming killers or addicts. Which one you gonna be, Shadow?"

"About the party," he said, changing the subject.

Millie rubbed her arm absently, as if she had just caught a chill. "It's kind of short notice. I ain't got the proper time to pull myself together."

"Mom sent a dress for you. I got it in the trunk of the car.

It might be a little baggy, though." He instantly regretted the comment about her weight; he wasn't trying to be mean. Her skinniness was simply impossible to ignore. "But I'll pay for it to get altered, if need be. Maybe even buy you a new one if you don't like what she sent." He pulled out his small bankroll to show Millie that he was holding.

Millie eyed the cash hungrily. Shadow was probably only working with a few hundred dollars at best, but that was more than enough to keep Millie on cloud nine for a good stretch. The addicted side of her brain told Millie to take the money, yet the big sister in her closed Shadow's hand around it to let him know she was refusing his offer. "Thanks, but I'm good," she said softly. Her baby brother was one of the few people Millie wouldn't take from, no matter the circumstances. Although she was strung out, she still held enough control over herself to put boundaries on her inner addict.

"Millie, this is important," Shadow said. "All Mom wants is for the King children to show a unified front."

"You mean she wants us to smile in front of the press and pretend to be an all-American family instead of the monsters we really are?" Millie said between laughs.

"Listen, I ain't about to stand here and beg you. You don't like my dad? I get that, but this isn't for him. It's for Mom. Don't shit on her just to spite him."

Millie folded her arms over her chest and grunted.

"I told Mom this trip would be a waste of time," Shadow mumbled, heading for the door, but Millie stopped him.

"I'll walk you to the car. You brought the dress all this way, the least I can do is try it on."

Shadow's eyes lit up.

"Don't be smirking at me like you did something slick. I'm not making any promises to show up, but I'm not saying that I won't either. Now, come on so I can see this dress, and it better not be ugly."

PART III

THE LAST SUPPER

CHAPTER 15

The early etchings of night fell as Shadow drove home. His trip to Brooklyn had proved more adventurous than he'd expected. After giving Millie the dress, he stayed around and kicked it with her for a while. Just as their time together took on the familiar air of the old days, her monkey started scratching her back again. She didn't say anything, but Shadow could tell; her movements became slightly jerkier and her nose started to run. He knew that she had what she needed with her and the only reason she wasn't getting high was out of respect for her little brother. So he made up an excuse to leave so she could get herself together. He still didn't know if she was planning on attending the party or not, but he was hopeful.

It was getting late and he still had a lot to do. He dropped Pain off first, in the projects, with the last of the rock that he had pinched from one of the King stash houses. This was their little hustle. Whenever Shadow could, he would tap one of the stashes for a bit of product. It was only shake, the crumbs left over from whenever one of their chefs cooked up a large batch of coke. The chefs usually saved the shake to bless loyal fiends who brought them business, but Shadow had a standing arrangement with some of the dudes who worked the houses. He'd throw them a few dollars to turn a blind eye while he helped himself. Shadow would give the crack to Pain and Fresh to hustle off. Shadow didn't do it for the money, he did it so his friends wouldn't starve. When he was older and in position, he intended to bring them into the family. Until that time came, however, he would do what he could to make sure things didn't get too hard for them.

Fresh didn't get out of the car with Pain. He claimed that he was going to slide over and see a chick who stayed on New York Avenue, but it felt more like he was trying to avoid the block. Likely because of what had gone down with Malice. Pain clowned him, but Shadow didn't.

On the way over to New York Avenue, Shadow passed a pawnshop. He found a nice necklace to grab as a present for his mom—she'd never have to know where it came from. Not that she would care, so long as her baby boy didn't show up empty-handed. *The child who never disappoints.*

Fresh was unusually quiet during the ride. Shadow tried to engage him in small talk, but it was obvious that something was troubling him. After a bit of probing, Fresh finally confided that he was indeed still concerned about a potential issue with Malice, but his family was also having some financial struggles at home. His mother worked two jobs, and he hustled, but they were still barely making ends meet. Shadow offered to speak to his parents about trying to help Irene get a better job, but Fresh's pride wouldn't allow it, nor would his mother's. Though Shadow's heart was in the right place when he made the offer, Fresh seemed to take it as a handout. He and his family would find a way, he said, and Shadow didn't press the issue. Before Fresh got out of the car, Shadow handed over what was left of his bankroll, along with his mother's gun. Loaning the derringer probably wasn't the smartest thing he had ever done, but he wanted Fresh to feel safe when he went home that night. It would only be for a day or two until Shadow could figure out something else. His mother didn't drive the Benz very often, so he was confident he could have the gun back in its hiding spot before she missed it.

When Shadow pulled up to his house, he found it alive with activity. The driveway was lined with so many vehicles that he had to park his mother's car on the street. He grabbed his tuxedo and his mother's gift from the backseat and hurried up the driveway. He nodded to a few of the soldiers standing guard, but didn't stop to exchange words. His father had called him three times and his mother once, likely wondering where the hell he was. Of course his mother knew, but he'd have to think of how to spin it to his father. Maureen had undoubtedly covered for him, but he had no way of knowing what tall tale she had cooked up. With any luck, he would be able to slip into the house and avoid his father, at least until he got dressed.

A white Escalade limo idled at the curb outside the house. This was the King family's flagship vehicle, and his dad only pulled it out for special occasions. Nefertiti leaned against the limo, which probably meant that she would be driving them that night. He wasn't surprised; she was always reluctant to let Lolli out of her sight. Normally, Shadow considered Nefertiti one of the guys, but now he did a double take. She wore a formfitting, knee-length skirt with a high slit. Her legs were well-oiled and a black blazer tightly hugged her chest, stopping just short of her thin waist. Shadow watched her tug at her fingerless gloves, and for a quick instant a fantasy popped into his head that made him lower his eyes in shame.

Standing there shooting the breeze with Nefertiti was Ghost's young protégé, Christian. Shadow knew that Christian was one of Ghost's favorite street lieutenants, but the fact that he had been invited to such a prestigious event said that his star was rising faster than anyone suspected.

Shadow fought back a chuckle when he took in the man's outfit. He wore full black coattails and gloves, and his cummerbund was dotted with silver sequins. The kicker of the outfit were his shoes. They were black and polished to a high shine, but the two-inch heels contained some sort of liquid. Upon closer inspection, Shadow realized that the heels were fashioned after snow globes. Full winter scenes took place in each, little figurines spinning amid falling snow. The dude looked like a cross between an orchestra conductor and a circus ringmaster.

"You gonna keep standing there gawking or you gonna speak?" Christian called out.

"Um . . . my fault. I was just checking out your outfit," Shadow managed to say without bursting into laughter.

"Whenever I step out, my drip has got to be serious, especially when I'm sitting amongst royalty," Christian said, popping his collar. He did a little turn so that Shadow could take in the whole outfit.

"You'll be sitting at the kiddie table with the rest of the junior members," Nefertiti chimed in, shoving Christian playfully.

"Listen, all you gotta do is let me in the room and I'll do the rest," Christian said. "The prince ain't never needed no hands up."

"Look, it wasn't easy for Ghost to convince his parents that you're ready for this step," Nefertiti said. "Maureen asked me if I cosigned the move and I said I did. That means both our reputations are on the line. I need you to check that diva shit at the door. I need your mouth shut and your ears open."

This was an interesting bit of news to Shadow. He knew of Ghost's connection to Christian, but what would make Nefertiti vouch for him?

"Well, I'd better get back to my ride," Christian said. "I don't want Ghost to see me out here fraternizing and put me back on the bench." He waved, pivoted on his heels, and walked off.

"That is one strange fruit," Shadow remarked. "I don't know what Ghost sees in him."

"No one does. That's what makes him so dangerous." Nefertiti looked at her watch and then back up at Shadow. "You're cutting it kind of close. We're supposed to be pulling out in the next few minutes."

"I had some business to take care of in Brooklyn and lost track of time."

Nefertiti studied his face. "Punctuality is a sign of good character. A man's character is all he has to stand on in this world."

"I'm not in your world?" Shadow said.

"Maybe not now." She cast a glance at the house. Ghost stood in the window watching them. "None of us can be sure what tomorrow holds until we get there." Nefertiti patted Shadow's shoulder, but there was something in her words that gave him the chills.

He shrugged and trotted off toward the house.

"Shadow," Nefertiti called after him, "next time have the common decency to wash up before you come back to the pad. You reek of weed."

Shadow nodded. Nefertiti was like a damn bloodhound.

As soon as he crossed the threshold he was met by Ghost, who wore a black tuxedo, similar to the one Shadow carried in his garment bag. Ghost looked tired and lines of worry streaked across his face.

"You good, big bro?" Shadow asked.

Ghost gave him a half smile. "I'm a King—we're good even when we ain't. But yo, where you been? Dad has been losing his shit looking for you."

"I slid into Brooklyn after school. Wanted to check up on the homies right quick." Shadow was pleased with this lie—it was only partially untrue.

Ghost looked at his watch. "You were able to go from school to Brooklyn and back in such a short time using public transportation?"

"I took an Uber back," Shadow answered, not wanting to betray his mother.

"Shadow, I'm gonna need you to steer clear of the old neighborhood for a while," Ghost told him.

"Why? Going to the hood is the only time I can see my friends and really have fun. You don't have to worry, Ghost. I know what's popping in the hood and I always make sure I'm careful."

"You don't know shit," Ghost said through clenched teeth. "If I'm asking you to stay away, I'm asking for a reason. Don't fight me on this, Shadow."

"Whatever, man," Shadow said, rolling his eyes. He wasn't in the mood for a lecture. He started to walk off, but the next thing he knew there was a vise grip around his neck. Ghost dragged him to a corner, slamming his back against the wall.

"You listen to me and you listen good, you spoiled little muthafucka," Ghost raged, spraying saliva across Shadow's face. "I ain't Pain, Fresh, or none of them other little niggas that treat you like you're Michael Corleone. Now, I've been letting you have your fun playing gangster in Brooklyn, with you side crack hustle and whatever else you're into." Shadow's eyes widened at the mention of the crack. "What? You think I didn't know? You ain't that slick, Shadow. While you're rolling your eyes and sucking your teeth like a little bitch, I'm trying to tell you something that may save your life." He gave his little brother a good shake. Seeing the fear in Shadow's eyes made Ghost soften his stance and release him.

"The hell is wrong with you?" Shadow said, shoving his brother, trying to rediscover his courage. He had never seen this side of his brother before—on edge and a little afraid.

"I'm sorry, Shadow," Ghost said, smoothing Shadow's clothes. "I didn't mean to come at you crazy, but I really need you to hear me on this. This shit with Daddy has everything fucked up. There's a lot going on right now that I really can't get into, but things are about to get insane, especially in the streets. Your friends Pain and Fresh? They live at ground zero of a war zone every day of their lives, so they know how to navigate it. You, I'm afraid, are going to go there one day and accidentally step on a land mine."

"Ghost, contrary to what everybody thinks, I'm not that naïve. I know there's something going on and it has to do with Dad running for office. Instead of lying to me about it, just keep it on the level."

Ghost placed his hands on Shadow's cheeks. "If only I could. Just know that whatever happens, I'm always gonna make sure our family is good. I just need you to trust me."

"Whatever you say." Shadow pulled away and headed to his room. What Ghost was doing was a prime example of why Shadow slid off to Brooklyn every chance he got. His brother and father wanted to shelter him to the point where he felt like a prisoner. How was he to just accept their bullshit? Maybe Millie was right. Nobody seemed to give a shit about what he thought or how he felt. Pain and Fresh might not have had nice homes or expensive cars, but at least they treated him like a person and not some fragile thing that could accidentally break at any given moment.

CHAPTER 16

S hadow showered and dressed in record time. He stood in front of his full-length mirror, admiring himself. The tuxedo fit him tighter than the last time he wore it, but the snugness showed off his body more, especially around the arms. Shadow flexed his biceps. He wasn't as well built as Ghost, but in time . . . in time.

He was hitting his braids with a bottle of spray-sheen when a knock fell at his door. "Yo," he answered. When the door opened and Shadow saw who was standing there, his stomach lurched.

"You're a hard man to catch up with," Chance said, stepping into the room and closing the door behind him. He also wore a tuxedo, yet his was silver. His bow tie hung untied around his neck and he held a cocktail in his hand.

"Were you trying to reach me? My fault—my phone died and I didn't have a chance to charge it until I got back to the house." The lie rolled effortlessly off Shadow's tongue. "Everything good?"

Chance sat on Shadow's bed and peered up at him. "I don't know. Is it?"

Shadow could feel his palms start to sweat. His father rarely asked a question he didn't already know the answer to. "What do you mean?"

"Your mother told me where you were today," Chance said.

The words hit Shadow like a slap. After all he had gone

through, his mother had given him up? "Dad, I can explain—" he began, but his father waved him silent.

"No need, son. Look, I get it. I was young once too. I had my fair share of struggles in school and never asked for help because I didn't want people looking at me like I was stupid. You ain't got those kinds off hang-ups. I'm proud of you, son, for taking the initiative to get after-school tutoring."

"I . . . um . . . thanks." Shadow wasn't sure what else he could say. Apparently, his mother had been on top of the situation after all.

"Listen, if you need me to shell out a few dollars to get you a private tutor, somebody who can come to the house if you feel some type of way about being seen getting the help at school—"

"No, I don't think that'll be necessary. I'm okay with getting help at school."

"Good man," Chance said, taking a sip from his drink. "So, you ready for tonight?"

"I should be asking you that. This is your big announcement."

"Yes, but it'll be an announcement that will affect this entire family. Especially you."

"Me? Dad, everybody knows that Ghost is your heir," Shadow said.

Chance stood and placed a hand on his son's shoulder. "Yes, Ghost is my heir, but you will be the future of this family." He paused, inhaled deeply, and stared directly into his son's eyes. "From the moment I first laid eyes on you in the hospital, I knew what you would become. It was the same with Ghost, and Lolli too. Your destinies were manifested the moment you came into this world. Ghost is my wrath, Lolli is my spirit, and you . . . you're my heart, Sean King. You are every part of me that is good and kind, and that's what this family will need going forward."

Shadow was stunned. His father couldn't possibly be preparing to offer him what he had been certain was meant for Ghost. "Dad, I'm honored that you'd consider me for this over Ghost, but—"

Chance lifted his hand to silence Shadow again. "Slow down, killer. All things involving the monarchy will pass to Ghost when my time is done. This you can be sure of."

"Then what's with this heavy conversation we're having like my role in this family is of any real importance?"

"Your position will be the most important one of all. You will be the family's last line of defense. If it turns out Ghost was the wrong way, you'll be the right one."

"Meaning?" Shadow thought he knew what his father was getting at, but he needed to hear him say it.

"Meaning your power won't come from being the prince of Five Points, it'll come from just being Sean King. Do you understand?"

"I think so," Shadow said, feeling like there was now even more pressure on him than when he'd thought his father was getting ready to offer him the crown.

"Good enough." Chance clapped him on the back. "Let me go check on your mom and make sure her slow ass is ready to boogie. Be outside in ten minutes so we can head out." He started for the door, then added, "In the event that something should happen to me, I want you to remember this conversation and your place in the family." He left without waiting for a response.

Five minutes passed before Shadow completed the challenge of tying his bow tie. He would've just gone with a clip-on, but he never would have heard the end of it from his father. One of the first things that Chance taught his son, besides how to shoot guns, was the art of tying different types of ties. Regular ties

Shadow could do with no problem; he was even fairly skilled with ascots. It was the bow ties that gave him trouble.

Between Ghost's behavior and his dad's cryptic words, Shadow was certain that something particularly serious was going on. The only other time in his life that he could remember the men in his family on edge like this was when they had gone to war with a rival organization. Shadow was fairly young at the time, but he could recall not being able to go outside and play beyond the backyard. Even the local park in their subdivision was off-limits. It was one of the few times he could remember his father being anything close to afraid. Could that be it? Were the Kings on the cusp of another war?

You're bugging, Shadow, he said to himself, patting his cheeks and trying to snap himself out of his thoughts. The days of open warfare in the streets were over, the monarchy had seen to that. So long as there was a king on the throne, the threat of his family going to war was slim to none.

After making sure his bow tie was straight, Shadow applied the finishing touches to his outfit. It wasn't enough for him to look like money, he had to smell like it too. He rummaged through the different bottles of cologne on his dresser until he found the one he was looking for: Creed. It was his favorite scent. Women went crazy when they smelled it on him, which was his aim with Orlando Zaza's daughter tonight.

Out of curiosity, he searched for Josette Zaza on social media. She didn't seem to have a Facebook or Twitter account, but he found her on Instagram. Her most recent picture, though, had been posted two years ago, a poor-quality shot of her shopping with some friends. She looked okay—long hair, decent figure, and a cute face—but nothing to write home about. Still, his mom had insisted that he be nice, so he would give her nice. By ten p.m., Shadow planned on having the girl in one of the bathrooms at the banquet hall with her legs in the air.

When he picked up the bottle of Creed he was disappointed to find it empty. He could've gone with another fragrance, but he had his heart set on Creed. There was no way he would be able to make a run to the mall to pick up more, but he did know where he could score some. Creed happened to be Lolli's favorite scent too, so he would just borrow from her.

He made his way down the hall to Lolli's room and knocked softly. He waited a few seconds but didn't hear a response. Knowing Lolli, she probably hadn't come home yet. She knew better than to miss her mother's birthday dinner, but it wouldn't be unlike her to show up late and probably tipsy. He envied his sister's life. Unlike the others, Lolli was a free spirit and did as she pleased.

When Shadow let himself into her room, he was surprised to find her sitting on the edge of her bed dressed in only a black bra, corset, and black slacks. She was stuffing what looked like soiled clothes into a plastic bag. Shadow couldn't be sure, but he thought he caught a flash of blood on one of the garments. She was so preoccupied with her task that she hadn't even heard him come in.

"What are you doing?" Shadow asked.

Lolli nearly jumped out of her skin at the sound of his voice. "Damn, don't you know how to knock?"

"I did, but nobody answered."

"Then you should've knocked again! What do you want, Sean?" Lolli asked, clearly trying to suppress the anxiety in her voice.

"I only wanted to borrow some of your cologne, but forget about it. I don't know what's going on with everybody in this house tonight, but I'm tired of being the whipping boy!" He started to stomp off.

"Wait, Shadow," Lolli called after him. "Look, I'm sorry about snapping at you. I've just got a lot on my mind."

"Seems like that's the theme with everybody today. I thought Ghost was gonna knock my head off earlier and Dad just left my room acting really strange, talking all cryptic and shit like he might not be around much longer."

Lolli seemed taken aback. "Sean, I want to talk to you. Close the door and come sit with me."

Shadow did as he was told and sat on the bed next to his sister. A coldness stained her normally playful eyes, a coldness that reminded him of Ghost. Shadow put his hand on his sister's knee and asked, "What's wrong Lolli? What am I missing that people keep trying to hide from me?"

"Change," she said flatly. "Dad is planning to vacate his throne and dive headfirst into politics, and there are people on both sides who aren't cool with this idea."

Shadow nodded; things were starting to make sense. "I can understand the monarchy being in their feelings about dad leaving, but them white boys that he plays politics with don't have any skin in the game. They've been okay with it up until this point, so why would they be against it now?"

"Let me paint a picture for you, little brother. A young man from the ghetto, born with nothing, pulls himself up by his bootstraps. Today, he wants to run for borough president, tomorrow he wants to be the mayor, and ten years from now? Maybe we find ourselves relocating to DC. Dad has become a threat because of what he represents. Chancellor King is on the cusp of living the American Dream. If he climbs high enough in office, it sends a message to every kid in the ghetto who comes from nothing that anything is possible. This makes him a threat to the good old boys in power. These people never want another Obama to ascend to the Oval Office, and I'm afraid they'll try to find a way to cut Daddy down to prevent it."

"Then we can't just sit and hope for the best," Shadow said. "We need to do something."

Lolli cast her eyes at the plastic bag by her feet. "I already have, though I'm afraid I might've hurt the situation more than helped."

"What did you do, Lolli?"

"Nothing for you to worry about. I just wanted to prove to Dad that I'm not useless just because I'm a girl."

Shadow placed his arm around his sister's shoulders. She turned away so that he wouldn't see the tears forming in her eyes, but he forced her to face him. "You're not useless, especially not to Daddy. He values you more than you give him credit for. Do you know what he calls you?"

Lolli raised her eyebrows.

Shadow placed a hand over his heart. "His spirit."

"Shut up. No, he didn't," Lolli said, smiling and shoving him.

Shadow raised his right hand. "Swear to God. I think we've been underestimating our father, Lolli. He sees us as valuable members of this family. I know that Ghost is the heir, but I suspect we'll all need to play our respective parts if we want to keep this family together."

Lolli laughed. "You sound like Uncle Colt."

"If only I was strong in the streets like he was," Shadow said, thinking of the Reapers. If they were still around, the Kings would have nothing to fear from their enemies, neither in the monarchy nor in politics.

"You may not have his mean streak, but you definitely have his heart. That'll serve you better than a gun. Remember I told you that."

"Right," Shadow said, nodding. "I better let you finish getting dressed before Mom comes up in here flipping."

"Aren't you forgetting something?" Lolli said, grabbing her Creed from the nightstand and tossing it to him. "Don't use up all my shit!"

"I got you." He walked to the door and rested his hand on the knob. "Do you think we should be worried?"

"Between me and you, Shadow, I'm *always* worried. That's the price we pay for being born into royalty."

CHAPTER 17

The ride to the venue was unusually quiet. Everybody seemed to be lost in their own thoughts. Ghost busied himself staring out the window, an agitated air hovering about him. Shadow wasn't sure if it had to do with what they had discussed at the house, or the fact that his fiancée, Kelly, hadn't bothered to attend the event with them. Shadow had never known the girl to miss an opportunity to grandstand with the royal family, so her being MIA was unusual. He was tempted to ask Ghost where she was, but decided against it—some things were better left alone. Ghost would talk about it when he was ready, or he wouldn't.

Shadow's parents did a good job of acting like everything was fine, but it wasn't hard to tell that something was going on between them. Chapman sat quietly, legs crossed and foot twirling, watching everyone from behind his sunglasses. Every so often he glanced in Shadow's direction and smirked, like he knew something that Shadow didn't and couldn't wait to tell it.

Lolli was the only one who acted as if she didn't have a care in the world. She raided the vehicle's minibar for nips of bourbon while scrolling through her phone. Lolli could drink with the best of them, but it wasn't like her to indulge so heavily before an event with their parents, especially a birthday. She normally waited until they got the formalities out of the way before getting shit-faced. She adjusted herself on the seat and Shadow thought he saw the handle of a gun sticking out from her garter belt.

"Don't get so drunk that you get in this place and show out," Chance warned her.

"I ain't getting drunk, I'm getting nice," Lolli said, rolling her eyes and helping herself to another nip.

"You sound like Millie," Chance joked. No one laughed.

Maureen and Shadow exchanged looks at the mention of Millie. Chance didn't seem to catch it, but Chapman did. Shadow could feel his uncle's eyes glued to him from behind those sunglasses. Shadow remembered Millie remarking on Chapman's love of gossip.

"C'mon, why all the long faces?" Chance said, his eyes sweeping over his children. "It's your mother's birthday, for crying out loud! We've got this nice venue, great food, and top-shelf liquor. Can we at least act like we're going to a party instead of a funeral?"

"Let them kids be, Chance," Maureen interjected.

"I, for one, am happy to be getting out of the house," Chapman said. "It's been far too long since the royal family has made a public appearance. I think it's long overdue that we remind people just who we are."

"This ain't about the monarchy, Chapman," Chance said. "This is about Maureen."

"Which would explain why all of your playmates got invitations, though half of them probably aren't going to show?" Evidently Chapman was in a shit-stirring mood. And while Chance wouldn't feed into it, his oldest son couldn't resist.

"Watch yourself, nigga," Ghost threatened. "You open your mouth out of pocket one more time and you're gonna find yourself in a bad way." With everything going on, Ghost was a powder keg that had yet to explode. He was clearly spoiling to hurt something.

"No, C.J., let the idiot speak," Maureen instructed. "It's

better to be thought of as a fool than to open your mouth and remove all doubt." Her eyes locked on Chapman. "You've had them forty-thousand-dollar fangs of yours bared all night and most of us here know why. I'll say this to you once and no more: You can keep snapping at the hands that feed you, if you have a mind to, or you can sink your teeth into the real enemy if and when the time comes."

"And who is our real enemy in all this, Madam Queen?" Chapman responded.

Maureen placed her hand on Chance's lap. "Any who would stand against my king."

Chapman couldn't help but be impressed by his sister-in-law's dedication. "*For richer and for poorer, in sickness and in health . . .*"

"*Until death do us part,* and you better damn well know it," Maureen finished, nestling herself against Chance.

Shadow watched in amusement as his mother and uncle traded swipes, his father helplessly trying to defuse the situation. It was better than a prime-time sitcom. His mom and Chapman were worse than oil and water; sometimes, Shadow thought that the only reason she hadn't tried to kill his uncle yet was out of love for his father. But he wouldn't put anything past Chapman.

Shadow's phone vibrated in his pocket, and he quickly fumbled for it. He looked at the screen and saw that it was Fresh. He was about to answer when Nefertiti's voice came over the intercom.

"We're here," she announced.

"Okay, y'all. It's time to get right," Chance said formally. "All petty grievances and squabbles we leave in this car. When we walk into this joint, we will present a unified front, even if it's just a front. Infighting is a sign of weakness, which is just what our enemies will be looking for. Afterward, y'all can go back to insulting each other or rehashing whatever bullshit you got going on. For the next few hours, though, we will be a family. All for the family." He extended his fist.

Nobody moved at first. Deadly glares were traded among the passengers and for a moment Chance thought that his words hadn't had the desired effect. Then, the most unlikely of the King children stepped up.

"All for the family," Shadow said, touching his fist to his father's. When his siblings still hesitated, Chance gave them a commanding look. One by one, Maureen and the siblings added their fists to the circle. Even Chapman finally joined them.

"All for the family," they said in unison.

Although no one knew it then, this was a turning point for the Kings.

CHAPTER 18

What started out as a shitty day for Malice turned around by sunset. He'd had the same routine for years: pick up, drop off, talk shit, and swallow spit. Since back when he was still in and out of jail and shooting at cats over petty bullshit, his career hadn't been very eventful. Of course, there was the occasional dustup, which was expected in his line of work, but it was rarely anything crazy. Yet Malice had really earned his stripes over the last few years. He had shot, cut, and stabbed enough niggas along the way to where he should not have been still proving himself, but every few years there would come a young upstart who sought to pull him out of character. Such was the case with the young East New York cat who called himself the Black Jew.

Malice had been aware of Judah for a while. He remembered when the dude was still getting burned on ounces of cocaine in Harlem, before he finally found the right plug. Even when Judah did get his feet under him, he stayed in his lane. Lately, though, he'd been swerving. The more he got his weight up, the bigger his eyes got. It wasn't long before he started stepping on toes, with the latest unfortunate dance partner being Malice. Judah was a kid who Malice had never really acknowledged, but when he started sniffing around what belonged to the older hustler, it moved him from the position of punk to an actual threat.

The sad part was that when Malice reflected on how they'd

gotten to this point, he had no one but himself to blame. He had gotten drunk and did some bozo shit, but he wanted to make it right in the way of a peace offering. This was why he had been trying to reach out to Ghost. The streets knew that Ghost was set to be the next king, so the last thing Malice needed was to be on his bad side. Ghost was in his feelings, but once he heard what Malice had to say, it would inevitably relieve some of the tension between them. In fact, Ghost would probably put him in position as a way of showing gratitude for Malice exposing the move that was about to be made against him. The streets were talking, and what they were saying wasn't good for the future king, or the current one for that matter. Malice needed to contact Ghost, but first he would have to deal with Judah, which was proving to be easier said than done.

Malice finished making his rounds by early evening. None of his spots were short that day, which was a good thing. After making his last pickup, he decided to head home. He and some of his crew were supposed to go out that night, so he needed to shower and change.

Before entering his building, he hit the store for some blunt wraps. The plan was to burn one while laying out his clothes. "Let me get a box of Dutch Masters," he told the man behind the counter, while also grabbing a six-pack from the cooler. When he rounded the aisle, he found himself confronted with a beautiful sight: a plump young ass in a pair of tight jeans bent over one of the coolers. Malice stood there for a moment, admiring the view. The girl must've felt his lecherous eyes because she turned around.

"I'm sorry, am in your way?" she asked in a voice that was as sweet as she looked. She was light-skinned, with long black braids and lips that looked like they were made for sucking dick.

"Nah, love. You good," Malice said, trying to sound sexy.

She gave him a smile and went back into the freezer, emerging with a six-pack of Corona. When she passed him to go to the counter, she made it a point to brush against him. Malice caught an instant erection. He *had* to taste that.

"Girl, you don't even look old enough to drink," Malice said, following her to the counter, forgetting about his own beers.

"I'm twenty-three," she said, sounding like she had picked the number out of thin air—not that Malice cared. "Besides, they aren't for me. They're for my auntie." She reached into her purse for cash, but Malice stopped her. He pulled out his bankroll and slowly began thumbing through it. He could feel her eyes on the money. The hook was baited and now all he had to do was reel her in. He slid the cash across the counter and retrieved the box of blunts while the girl grabbed her beers.

"Such a gentleman," she said.

"I've been called a lot of things by women, but I don't think gentleman is one of them," Malice joked.

"Then maybe you've been hanging around the wrong type of broads."

"And you're the right kind?"

The girl shrugged.

"Listen, I don't know what you got planned right now, but I was about to go to my crib and burn one. I stay right up the block."

"I'm down for that. I just have to drop these beers off to my auntie. She stays around the corner. You wanna walk with me, then we can go back to your place?"

"Bet," Malice said, holding the store's door open for her. "What's your name, lil' mama?"

"Chelsea."

Chelsea and Malice walked down the block, chatting like two

old friends. She told Malice how she had just moved to the neighborhood to stay with her aunt on account of her not getting along with her mom. That would explain why he had never seen her in the area. Every few feet, she made it a point to touch him, or rub up against him. Malice was primed and couldn't wait to get her back to his apartment and split her open.

"This is it," Chelsea said, stopping in front of a seedy-looking building.

Malice looked up at the building. It was a wreck and should've been condemned a long time ago. He passed this building all the time, but didn't think anybody other than crackheads stayed there.

"You don't have to go in with me if you don't want to," she said. "I can run the beers upstairs and meet you back here."

"Nah, I'll go with you," he mumbled. The last thing Malice wanted was for her to get to her aunt's house and change her mind about him. He wasn't letting the young girl out of his sight until he smashed. He held the cracked glass door for her and followed behind her.

The inside of the building looked just as bad as the outside. Overhead, a naked light bulb winked on and off, painting the foyer in eerie shadows. The hallways stank of piss and cigarette smoke. The walls were cracked and marked with gang graffiti. It was a cesspool, and if Chelsea was staying there with her aunt, he was going to make her jump in the shower before he allowed her to touch his sheets. Just being inside the building made him itch, and the sooner Malice was able to get out of there, the better.

When Malice let the door swing shut behind him, it bumped his hand, causing the box of Dutch Masters to fall on the ground. When he bent over to pick it up, he heard a loud bang, followed by what was left of the lobby door's glass shattering. Someone one was shooting—at him. His eyes darted up, and he spotted a man in a hoodie on the stairs, holding a smoking gun. The little bitch had set him up!

Malice abandoned his blunts and drew his weapon. The shooter in the hoodie was closing on him. Before Malice could pull the trigger, Chelsea swung the bag holding the six-pack. The bottles shattered, spraying glass and beer all over Malice, causing him to lose his grip on his pistol. There was a second shot, followed by an explosion of pain in his shoulder. Malice's survival instincts kicked in and he took off running.

He made it half a block before his arm started going numb. He was bleeding like a stuck pig, leaving a trail of red behind him. A quick glance over his shoulder told him that the shooter was still with him. Malice had gotten a head start, but the man was gaining. The hoodie obscured his face, though Malice was pretty sure it was Judah. With one arm and no weapon, he was dead in the water, so he ran faster.

Malice just reached his building when another shot was fired. This one narrowly missed his face, sparking off the side of the building. He tried to pull his key out of his pocket, but his fingers wouldn't cooperate. He was sweating, and starting to get dizzy. Likely from all the blood he was losing. The shooter was almost on him, moving in like a predatory cat. Malice realized he was about to die.

Just then, fate tossed him a bone. One of the tenants, an old woman, stepped out of the building. He damn near knocked her over when he rushed inside. With his last bit of strength, he pulled the door closed behind him. The hooded man tried to snatch it open, but it was locked. In frustration he then removed his hood so that Malice could see his face. Sure enough, it was Judah. Thinking about how close he had almost come to dying made Malice chuckle. Judah looked pissed, so Malice decided to rub salt in the wound and give him the finger. Little bastard had almost caught Malice slipping—*almost*. Judah wouldn't get a second chance, this he was sure of.

When Malice turned to head up the stairs, he found himself confronted with another familiar face. This one wore no hood; he wanted Malice to see him.

Malice sighed. "It's always the quiet ones you gotta watch."

Those were the last words he ever spoke.

CHAPTER 19

As he led the procession into the banquet hall, Chancellor King received what could only be described as a king's welcome. Every man and woman in the room rose to their feet and clapped in respect for the king and queen. Chance looked quite regal in his tuxedo with a gold crown pinned to the lapel. On his arm, Maureen was no less stunning in her black sequin ball gown. Her wrists, fingers, ears, and neck were adorned with so many stones that when the light kissed them she seemed to shimmer. Atop her head was a diamond tiara.

Chippie came over to meet the family. She looked different with her hair done and makeup on. She had even ditched her glasses for the night and gone with a pair of contacts. Her cocktail dress hugged her, but it wasn't tight. She showed off her figure without being too revealing. Clutched in her hand was her ever-present iPad. "Don't you all look sharp," she said warmly.

Chance kissed her on the cheek. "You ain't looking too bad yourself."

"I've got a few things that I need to float around and take care of, but we're all set." Chippie motioned for the family to follow her. "Let me get you guys to the table."

As they crossed the room, Maureen stopped to speak to a friend. Ghost waited, but the rest of them kept moving. Shadow and Lolli fell in step behind Chance. Shadow worked the room, smiling and winking at some of the women in attendance. Lolli walked beside her father and Chippie, eyes sweeping the room, as if she was expecting some type of threat to materialize.

"Are all the important people here?" Chance asked.

Chippie tapped the screen on her iPad and scrolled through the guest list. "For the most part, yes. The only people of note who seem to be missing are Mr. Salvatore and Alderman Porter."

Chance stopped walking. "I talked to Rocco personally, so that's no surprise, but I expected Porter to be here." He had spoken to the alderman, who had assured him that he wouldn't miss the event, though Chance had picked up on a hint of sarcasm.

"I'll let you know if he does show up," Chippie said.

When the Kings reached their table, they found it already partially occupied. Of course, Little Stevie was present at the King table. He wasn't blood, but was more family than some who shared the same DNA.

Sitting at the head of the table, a seat reserved for Chancellor, was a man dressed in a white suit with no tie. His face was dark and sun-beaten, and his thick hair was slicked back and lathered with way too much gel.

As Shadow studied his face, he realized why the name Zaza had sounded so familiar. This wasn't the first time he had laid eyes on Orlando Zaza. Shadow could vaguely remember seeing the man's face at their apartment in Brooklyn, and also at their new home. But Shadow hadn't seen him in at least three years.

Orlando Zaza was a major player. A Cuban native, he had made his bones in Miami. Over the last few years, he had built a power structure in New Jersey. He was the plug when it came to guns, fleecing his Cuban connect for as many firearms as he could handle, which he snuck in through Port Newark. The gun industry had made Orlando rich and he needed a way to launder all his dirty cash. This was how he'd originally met Chancellor King. For a small fee, Chance taught him how to launder his money through properties. He helped Orlando tap into a franchise of wireless phone retailers and soon the venture blossomed. To date, he had ten locations across New York, New Jersey, and Florida. Between the wireless stores and his gun business, Orlando did quite well for himself, though he still wanted more. What he really desired was a seat at Chance's table. Not at the birthday dinner—the *real* table. The monarchy.

"Looks like somebody didn't read the seating chart," Lolli said.

Orlando's jovial brown eyes turned to her. "Is that little Lollipop?" he said, standing. "The last time I saw you, you were still riding dirt bikes and skinning your knees. You're all grown up now."

"Nice to see you again, Mr. Zaza," Lolli said with a forced smile, extending her hand.

Orlando pulled Lolli into an uncomfortable hug. "We've got far too much history to be so formal."

"You better not let your wife see you making eyes at my baby girl," Chance half joked. He hadn't missed the intimacy of the hug.

Orlando placed his hand over his heart. "Ah, but if only I were twenty years younger. We'd run away together and leave my poor Juliette an old maid."

"And Shadow," Chance said, practically shoving his son to the forefront.

Shadow nodded awkwardly, not feeling how his father had put the attention on him. "Hi, Mr. Zaza."

"*Mr. Zaza* is for men who beg for my mercies. You can call me Orlando." He winked and held the boy's grip a little longer than needed.

"Cut that kind of chatter around Shadow," Chance interjected. "He ain't from that."

"No, that would be the other son," Orlando said, turning to Ghost, who had been staring daggers at him during the whole exchange. "What's the matter? The last time we saw each other, fire shot from your tongue, and tonight you can't find it?"

"Orlando," Ghost said flatly. An awkward silence lingered between them.

"Well, Orlando—hello!" Maureen chirped as she approached the table, breaking the tension. "I'm so glad you and your lovely family could make it tonight."

"When a friend calls," Orlando said, "I answer. Friendship is something that I value very deeply, as I'm sure the Kings already know."

"Indeed I do," Chance said, "and I'm looking forward to our friendship blossoming to something greater than what it was before."

Orlando didn't respond. Instead, he turned to his attention back to Maureen. "Happy birthday, Madam Queen." He took her hand and kissed the back of it.

"Thank you, Orlando," Maureen curtsied. "Where's that beautiful wife of yours?"

Orlando motioned across the room toward a bronze-colored woman with blond hair. "She and Josette are just over there. No doubt trading gossip."

"I must go over and say hello," Maureen said. "Come with me, Sean." When they got out of earshot, Maureen pulled her son close. "You do what I asked you?"

"Yeah, but I can't make any promises," Shadow said. "You know how Millie is."

"Only too well."

"That Orlando is an interesting character."

"Interesting? That's hardly the word I'd use to describe him. That whole Zaza clan is a nest of vipers."

"Then why is Dad doing business with him?"

Maureen shook her head. "A necessary evil. But Orlando isn't your concern tonight. Keep your eyes on the prize."

The short walk to where the Zaza women stood might as well have been the green mile. Juliette's hazel eyes were locked on Maureen the whole time. She looked like a retired movie star in her diamonds and perfectly painted face. The white dress she wore was so tight that it was a wonder she could breathe in it, let alone move. It dipped low in the front, showing off way too much cleavage, yet Maureen had to admit that the woman looked damn good for her age. It was no surprise, though, considering all the money her husband had spent on her cosmetic surgeries over the years.

Maureen put on her best plastic smile. "Hey, girl," she said, kissing the woman's cheek. "Been a long time."

"Three years, six months, and four days," Juliette said, flashing her perfect white teeth.

"Really? Seems like only yesterday."

Maureen and Juliette had never really gotten along. Even before the falling out between their husbands, the women's relationship had been turbulent. Perhaps because they were so much alike, two strong-willed queens with dominant personalities.

"I guess time flies when you're building empires," Juliette said cheerily, lifting her hand so that Maureen could see the diamonds on her fingers.

"I see Carmen didn't come with you guys," Maureen said, referring to the Zazas' oldest daughter.

"Regretfully, no. But she did ask me to wish you a happy birthday. She's actually on a honeymoon cruise with her new husband."

"Well, I'm glad she's found her soul mate. Please extend a congratulations on behalf of the royal family." Maureen could tell that the remark cut Juliette, which had been her intention.

"I doubt she would've come anyhow, all things considered," the woman said. "Oh, before I forget." She reached into her expensive handbag and withdrew an envelope, which she passed to Maureen. "Happy birthday from the Kingdom of Zaza."

Maureen clutched the envelope to her chest. "You shouldn't have."

"We had to. It isn't much, just a little something on your special day to show how much love and respect we have for the Kings." Juliette peered behind Maureen at Shadow and widened her smile. "And who is this fine slice of midnight you're hiding back there?"

"This is my youngest boy, Sean," Maureen said.

"Charmed." Juliette extended her hand, expecting Shadow to kiss it. Instead, he shook it. "He's just a darling, isn't he, Josette?"

The princess of the Zaza clan silently considered Shadow. He felt like a baby fawn in the crosshairs of a hungry cheetah. The smaller animal knew it was about to die, but for some reason couldn't will its legs to flee. Shadow was immediately both intrigued and frightened by Josette. She sure didn't look like the girl he'd seen on Instagram. She'd put on about fifteen pounds in all the right places, and he couldn't be sure, but from the way her tits sat perked up beneath the plunging neckline of her dress, it looked like she'd had some work done. He was relieved when Chippie unknowingly rescued him.

"Can everyone take their seats?" Chippie said. "Dinner is about to be served."

Shadow made his way back to the head table, with the

three women trailing behind him. When he glanced back, Josette was still staring at him like something wild and hungry. If nothing else, he knew it was going to be an interesting night.

CHAPTER 20

R ight before dinner was served, Shadow was thrown a curveball. Instead of sitting near the head of the table with his father and brother, he was told to sit with the Zaza family, right next to Josette. To his father's right, where Shadow would normally be sitting, was Orlando, who spent half the night laughing, hoisting glasses, and keeping people hanging on his every word. Shadow had to admit that there was something magnetic about the man's personality, but he also had a sharp edge to him. It was very subtle, but it was there.

Halfway through the meal, Shadow's phone vibrated in his pocket. It was Fresh again. He was about to answer when Mrs. Zaza started up a new conversation with him. She was quite the character. Almost everything that came out of her mouth had to do with either her own accomplishments or those of her family. She was a shallow woman, Shadow observed, who reminded him a lot of Uncle Chapman. In between her brags, she kept making remarks pertaining to Shadow and her daughter: how cute they'd be together, and so on and so forth. If Shadow didn't know any better, he would've thought that she was trying to play matchmaker.

Josette's personality was not quite as vibrant. Every five minutes or so she rolled her eyes and sighed loud enough for Shadow to hear. Even when he tried to engage her in small talk, her responses were short and half-hearted. She was about as interesting to Shadow as sunset was to a blind man. He was trying to think up an excuse to escape her when suddenly there was a shift.

It came around the time Juliette excused herself to use the bathroom. Josette waited for her mother to disappear into the hall before dropping her previous posture. She turned to Shadow and said, "Jesus, I thought she'd never stop talking! I'm sorry if my mother was embarrassing you."

"Nah, you're good," Shadow said. "She just wants the best for her daughter."

Josette studied him briefly before speaking. "You know, something I've noticed about you tonight is that you have a slightly inflated sense of self-importance. How does that crown fit on such a large head?"

Shadow was caught off guard by her sudden change of speed. He found himself momentarily at a loss for words.

"Relax," she said, "I'm only joking. You're confident. That's a good quality in a man." She smiled playfully and glanced around the room. "Let me ask you something. Where can a girl go for a bit of privacy?"

"Excuse me?" Shadow replied.

"I mean for this." She dipped her hand into her bra and produced a joint. "Do you burn?"

"Like a California brush fire!"

"While Mrs. Chatterbox is gone, let's get blazed right quick. Unless, of course, the king and queen need you to be in their line of vision at all times?"

"You must not know who you're talking to," Shadow said, standing and helping Josette up from her seat like a gentleman. "Follow me. I saw a dumpster around back that'll provide the perfect cover."

The adults were so busy getting drunk and having a good time that no one even noticed as the two teenagers headed for the exit. Moving with skill that could've only been born from experience, Josette snatched a bottle of whiskey from the bar on their way out the door. She was so smooth that the bartender didn't even notice.

In the recesses of the dumpsters, Shadow and Josette Zaza smoked a joint and drank whiskey straight from the bottle. Although her weed wasn't quite on the same level as the shit he'd smoked with Pain, he was nonetheless impressed with the strain.

Once the liquor and weed started working their way into their systems, Josette began opening up a bit. She told Shadow what it was like growing up as the youngest child of the Zaza family, about the expectations placed upon her and constant comparisons to her older sister, Carmen. This was why she put on an air of being prim and proper when she was around her parents—she had to be perfect at all times.

Shadow related to her story, except for the part about her being involved in the family business. Whereas Shadow's dad tried to keep him sheltered from the dirty side of the family operation, Josette had been pulled in all the way. She, not Carmen or their brother, was next in line to succeed their father.

"How do you deal with it?" Shadow asked. "Living in the shadow of something greater than yourself?" In the back of his mind, he was thinking about the dynamic between himself, his father, and Ghost.

"By reminding myself every day that nothing is greater than me," she declared. "Not my father, not my siblings, not even the Zaza name. I am the mistress of my own fate."

"So you're cool with being a part of the family business?"

"I'm looking forward to it," Josette said. "The business is my family's legacy. I know what my father has sacrificed to bring us to where we are. Why would I not want to make sure that, for generations, the Zazas are financially set? If I have to spill a little blood in the process, as long as it isn't Zaza blood, it is what it is."

"That's cold," Shadow said, chuckling.

"That's my life. You mean to tell me that you aren't looking forward to the day when you have to step up for your family?"

"That isn't exactly my lane. Ghost is heir to the throne."

"Sean, I'm not talking about a social club of old mobsters and cooks that everyone, including my father, wants so desperately to be a part of. I mean the real seat of power. The one our parents sending us to the best schools are preparing us to handle. If there's one thing I know about these old men who we come from, it's that they always plan ahead. Nothing is done without careful execution. Why do you think there was so much pressure on us to hook up tonight?"

"I don't follow you," Shadow said.

Josette slapped her forehead in frustration. "Sean, you can't be that oblivious to what's going on between our families, can you?"

Before Shadow could respond, his phone rang again. This time it was Pain. When he made to answer it, Josette snatched the phone away.

"That's rude, you know. Here we are having a deep conversation and you're about to get on your phone."

"Quit playing. That's one of my guys. I wanna make sure everything's okay." Shadow reached for his phone, but she held it just out of his reach.

"Unless this is a call about money or blood, I think your guys will be okay," Josette chided, clearly feeling the effects of the whiskey and weed. She held the phone behind her back, glassy eyes challenging him to come and take it. He did.

They tussled for a moment and he ended up pressing Josette against the wall behind the dumpster. They were so close that they could taste each other's breath. That hungry look returned to Josette's eyes and now that Shadow had a buzz he was up for the game. An invisible magnet seemed to pull them together, which they resisted at first. Eventually, however, they gave in and their lips connected. They sucked on each other's lips as if trying to draw juice from a fruit. Shadow felt her hand slip between his legs. He was hard as a rock.

"Nice," Josette breathed into his mouth, squeezing his dick with one hand and steering his hand under her gown with the other. She navigated Shadow's fingers inside her. When she took them out they were slick with her juices. Locking eyes with him, she took his hand and licked his fingers clean. "You wanna fuck me, don't you?"

In response, Shadow undid his belt and shoved his pants down around his hips. His dick popped out like a dangerous weapon, swollen with blood and tight. He felt like he would pop if he didn't have her. Shadow damn near foamed at the mouth when she turned her back to him and hiked up her gown. She wasn't wearing underwear. Josette placed one hand on the wall and the other between her legs, and started playing with her pussy. Shadow pressed himself against her and began running his dick back and forth over her pussy. It was so wet that it slipped right in. Shadow's eyes rolled back in his head as she closed her walls around him. He was barely five pumps in and felt like he was ready to bust.

Josette felt Shadow's dick thicken and began to open and close herself, teasing him. When she felt him tense, she pulled herself off him with a moist sound, grabbed a fistful of Shadow's braids, and kissed him again.

Shadow's strong hands wrapped around her thin waist and he lifted her onto her tiptoes. His dick found her pussy as if it had a homing beacon. Her eyes were closed and waves of pleasure rolled over her face. "The world will bow at our feet," she moaned into his ear. Shadow had no clue what she meant, nor did he care. All he could think about was her moist hole. Josette's pussy was so good that Shadow wanted to take up residence in it. He had her back pressed firmly to the wall and was working her—in . . . out . . . in . . . out. He happened to look at Josette's face and no longer were her eyes closed in the throes of passion. They stared at something just out of his line of vision. When he heard the sound of a bag hitting the ground, he knew that they weren't alone. Shadow prayed that he wouldn't turn around and find his mother, or worse, Mr. Zaza, standing behind him. What he found waiting for him behind door number three was even worse than the first two choices.

At first, he didn't recognize her. She was dressed in a plain white shirt and black pants, same as the rest of the waitstaff who had been hired to serve at the party. Her wig was gone, replaced with fresh box braids pulled into a ponytail. The trash bag she had come to toss in the dumpster now lay at her feet, loose garbage falling from its mouth. Tears danced in her eyes at the sight of Shadow thrusting into the Cuban girl. Of all the people he thought he might bump into at his mother's birthday party, Voodoo had not been one of them.

Voodoo's hand went to her mouth in embarrassment. She shook her head as if trying to dislodge the image of what she was witnessing. When the first tear rolled down her cheek, she turned and hurried back inside.

Shadow tried to pull his pants up. His dick was still hard and he was having trouble tucking it back into his underwear. Holding his pants up at the waist, he ran after Voodoo.

"Wait, did you just jump out of my pussy to go and chase the help?" Josette furiously called after him.

* * *

He finally caught up with Voodoo in the hallway.

"Leave me alone, Shadow," she said without stopping. She was crying and didn't want him to see.

He grabbed her by the arm, but she snatched it away. "Let me explain," he said.

"Don't you dare put your hands on me! You probably didn't even wash them after you climbed out of her nasty pussy!"

"Why don't you relax and let me explain," Shadow said.

"Explain what? That you were fucking that chick behind the dumpster like the trash she is? I knew all that shit you were talking earlier about being sorry for how things played out between us was bullshit. You still the same dog-ass nigga"

Shadow sighed. "Voodoo, I ain't even gonna front like you didn't just catch me jumping off out there, but what was I supposed to do? Wait until you got around to deciding if I was worthy of a second chance? I had no way of knowing where we are with this."

"You're absolutely right, Shadow. It's my own fault for thinking that maybe you were starting to mature enough to have finally figured it out. I can't believe I was actually thinking about letting your creep ass back into my life."

At that moment, Josette came walking down the hallway. She looked pissed and half-drunk. She slowed her pace and gave Voodoo a dirty look, then took a final swig from the bottle before pouring the rest of the liquor on the floor. "Might want to get somebody to clean that up," she said, laughing as she moseyed back into the banquet hall. Voodoo was about to go after her but Shadow stopped her.

"Chill, Voodoo," Shadow said. "You're better than that."

"You know what? You're right, I am better than that. I'm better than this . . ." she motioned around the hall, "and I'm for damn sure better than you."

A beefy black man wearing a white chef's coat and hat came into the hallway. When he spotted Voodoo, his face turned sour. "Williams, what the hell are you doing? You're not getting paid to socialize, you're being paid to bus tables!"

That was the last straw for Voodoo. "You know what? Fuck you and fuck this job!" she yelled. "And especially fuck you, Shadow!"

Shadow didn't try to stop her. He knew he had fucked up bad this time. What were the odds that the girl he truly loved would work at the same place he was fucking a random chick behind a dumpster? Voodoo was a good girl and he just kept fucking things up with her. Maybe it wasn't meant to be.

Shadow shuffled down the hall, thinking about what had just transpired. He had the urge to call an Uber and head home; he didn't want to party anymore. But then Uncle Chapman came out of the banquet room looking for him.

"Boy, where have you been?"

"I'm not in the mood for no bullshit right now," Shadow said.

"Your dad sent me to find you. They're about to bring out your mother's cake."

"I'll be there in a minute," Shadow muttered in a shaky voice.

Chapman gave him a look. He knew the signs—the sagging shoulders and eyes on the verge of tears. Yes, his nephew was suffering from a broken heart. "You good?" he asked.

"Not really," Shadow replied. He went on to tell the story of what had just happened with Josette and Voodoo. He wasn't sure why he was spilling his guts to Chapman, except for the fact that he needed to get it off his chest and any listening ear would do.

"My poor nephew," Chapman said, shaking his head.

"You've really managed to step in it, haven't you? I understand where you're coming from, and my heart goes out to you, but let me be honest. Bitches like Voodoo are a dime a dozen. Sure, she's cute, a true rider, and probably throws that young pussy like a grand champion, yet she's no Josette Zaza. Voodoo represents your past, but Josette represents what could be a very bright future for you and this family."

"Why the hell is everybody trying to push me off on this crazy Spanish broad?" Shadow snapped. Then he remembered what Millie had told him about Ghost. He was slowly trying to figure out where this was going, but needed one more piece of the puzzle to be sure. "Chapman, what did Dad try to do to Ghost and what does it have to do with what's going on tonight?"

Chapman wasn't surprised by the question. He had been waiting for it to come. In fact, he was a bit disappointed that his nephew hadn't asked him sooner. "Nephew," he said, draping his arm around Shadow, "walk with me while I give you a quick history lesson."

CHAPTER 21

Ten minutes after arriving, Ghost wished the event would hurry up and end. He suffered through it for the sake of his mother, but neither the party nor the guests were his scene. It was a room filled with fake-ass people bending over to kiss his father's butt. Not because they actually had love for him, but because they needed something from him.

Every so often he caught Orlando looking at him, smirking. He wanted to get up and slap the expression off his face, but he wouldn't take the bait. Ghost didn't like Orlando Zaza, though he understood the importance of the man's relationship with his father. Orlando had powerful friends in the Cuban government and these friends could help Chance's efforts to one day make it to Washington, DC. Ghost had been opposed to his father getting back into bed with Zaza and had told him so. He had never trusted Orlando, and trusted him even less after the incident that had soured their relationship in the first place. Ghost was largely to blame for it, and he accepted that. It just didn't sit right that all these years later, when Chance was on the cusp of pulling off one of the greatest moves of his career, Orlando had decided that he wanted to play nice again. It didn't seem genuine, yet the king didn't want to hear Ghost's concerns. He was so focused on all the pros that came with getting back into bed with the Zazas that he'd neglected the cons. Chance was determined to make the deal work, no matter what the costs—even to his own blood.

Orlando wasn't the only one who seemed off, though. Ever since Shadow had snuck off and come back, he sat among the Zazas with a sour look on his face. The girl didn't appear to be having a good time either. Before they crept out, Shadow and Josette had been snickering and whispering like two school kids, but now they hardly looked at each other. What had happened? When the brothers made eye contact, Ghost raised his glass in salute, to which Shadow responded by twisting his lips and averting his gaze. Shadow then caught the attention of a passing waiter and grabbed a drink from the platter he carried. Shadow wasn't a big drinker, but he was throwing them back tonight. Something was going on with his little brother, and Ghost made a note to himself to have a conversation with him later on.

His phone went off and he answered with an attitude: "Speak."

"It's me," Monster said on the other end.

"Everything okay? I'm kind of in the middle of something," Ghost told him. Across the room he watched Uncle Chapman whisper into the ear of a man Ghost didn't recognize. He wouldn't have noticed had the man not looked so out of place. He wore a sweater and Timberlands at what was supposed to be a black-tie event. How had he even gotten in dressed like that?

"Sorry to bother you, Cuz, but I figured you'd wanna get this news hot off the presses. That little problem we had ain't a problem no more."

"Good. The young boy came around and handled his business like I told you he would. See, you worried about nothing. All he needed was a little motivation to get on his job."

"I still don't know the details of what happened," Monster said, "but it's been confirmed that the strip is one man shorter as of this evening."

"One less bitch we gotta worry about," Ghost said, referencing his favorite N.W.A. song. "A'ight, get with me when you find out the details."

"Wait a second. One more thing I need to run by you. I spoke to the Lone Ranger." The name was code for a cop who Ghost had on payroll. He wasn't an agent of the King family; he answered directly to Ghost.

"And?" Ghost said. Monster stayed silent. "Speak, nigga!"

"This ain't really a conversation I want to have on the phone, but fuck it. You remember that thing I was asking you about? The *problem* that Uncle Chance needed solved?"

"What about it?" said Ghost.

"Well, as it turns out, the mess wasn't totally cleaned up. Word is there was a witness who can identify the shooter."

Ghost experienced a sinking feeling, but he kept his thoughts to himself and played it cool. "And why are you telling me this?"

"C'mon, Cuz. We've known each other all our lives. You really gonna play this game with me?" Ghost didn't respond, so Monster continued: "I'm telling you this because when they asked the witness who the killer was, he said, 'A ghost.'"

Ghost almost dropped his phone. Impossible! The word exploded in Ghost's head. He had been extremely careful with the hit he'd made on Freddy. There hadn't been anyone on the street, and even if there had been, Ghost would've sent them along for the ride. This was an unforeseen loose end that would need to be tied up ASAP. "Do we know who this witness is?"

"Yeah, some kid who happened to be sitting by his living room window when it went down. He saw the whole thing."

"He's gotta go," Ghost responded.

"Did you hear me when I said that the witness is a kid?"

"Whenever there's a choice between us and them, it's always gonna be them," Ghost told his cousin.

"That's some cold shit, Ghost. I've done a lot of dirt for you and this family, and I never once questioned an order, but this . . ." Monster removed the phone from his ear and bit hard on his bottom lip. As a parent himself, was he really down with killing a kid? "Look, this is something we need to talk about face-to-face."

"What the fuck is there to talk about?" Ghost said. "I told you what needs to be done. All for the family, right?"

Monster didn't say anything.

"You hear me?" Ghost barked.

"Yeah, I hear you," Monster muttered before ending the call.

As soon as Monster hung up, Ghost realized he had handled the situation wrong. For as long as he and Monster had run together, Monster had followed Ghost's lead like a faithful puppy. Monster was Uncle Colt's only son, but hadn't inherited his charisma and leadership qualities. What Monster lacked in initiative, though, he made up for in execution. The boy loved to get his hands dirty and had been one of Ghost's, and his father's, most important chess pieces. Monster had unquestioningly done Ghost's bidding for so long that sometimes the oldest King child took his cousin's services for granted. But the fact that Monster seemed to be questioning Ghost's recent decisions suggested that he was losing sway over his brutish cousin. Ghost knew that if he wanted to soothe the savage beast, it would take a show of good faith. Nothing small either. It would have to be something that would convince Monster that Ghost was at least trying to level the playing field between them, even if he really wasn't. The neighborhood they'd just taken from Malice might be sufficient. Of course, Judah wouldn't be happy about it, since he had put in the work and to him it was promised, but Ghost needed Monster more than he needed Judah.

He would find some other bone to throw the upstart. It was a cruddy move, but at the end of the day, Monster was family and Judah wasn't.

Chance tapped a fork against his champagne glass. Once he was sure that everyone in the banquet hall was focused on him, the king stood.

"Family," Chance began, "is a word that is thrown around far too loosely, but I use it here tonight because that is how I view each and every one of you in this room. Whether we share blood or not, we are all family, bound by deeds, love, and honor. As you all know, we have gathered here tonight for two very special occasions. The first, and most important, is my wife's birthday. I won't embarrass her by telling you her age—"

"You better not," Maureen chimed in. Laughter echoed around the room.

Chance smiled and touched his wife's shoulder. "What I will tell you is that it is a milestone birthday. When I met Maureen I was a young man still trying to find my way in the world. You, baby, became my guiding light. All these years you've given me encouragement when I was uncertain, counseled me through very tough decisions, and been my strength at times when I felt like I wasn't powerful enough. I can say with certainty that I would not be where I am today without you. For this, I am thankful." He bent over and kissed her on the lips. "Happy birthday to the love of my life. I wish you many more."

The room filled with cheers, claps, and birthday shouts. Maureen couldn't help but blush at the bountiful love and adoration. She truly felt like a queen.

"The second thing we're here to celebrate," Chance continued, "is the reason you're all scraping those forks over those five-thousand-dollar plates. Don't worry, though. The cash you so graciously parted with ain't going into my pockets. Your generosity has made you all official contributors to my new campaign. I am pleased to officially announce that I will be running for the office of Brooklyn borough president!"

The banquet hall erupted in applause, but Chance quickly motioned for them to quiet down.

"This is only the beginning," he said. "I won't bore you with the details, but just know that I have no plans to stop with the office of borough president. When it's all said and done, one of your own will walk the halls of our nation's capital. I do this for you, my family. All for the family." He raised his glass.

"For the family!" cheered the room.

It was a joyous moment, but short-lived. The room's attention turned from Chance to the front door, where a disturbance had suddenly erupted. It looked like security was trying to stop a party crasher from getting in. She was a haggard-looking woman, wearing a ball gown two sizes too big. Whoever this was would surely be on the receiving end of her bad decision to try and crash an event reserved for the Kings. But upon closer inspection, those in the know realized that the party crasher was, in fact, a King.

Maureen jetted over to the front door. She elbowed her way through the growing crowd of onlookers, moving so fast that she stepped on her dress and ripped it, but she didn't care. One of her babies was in trouble.

"Get your damn hands off me!" Millie yelped, struggling against the security guards, who were attempting to wrangle her out of the hall and back onto the street.

"Ma'am, we're going to need you to relax before this situation turns ugly," an overzealous security guard said, pulling out a can of pepper spray and holding it out at the irate young woman.

"If you don't get your hands off my daughter, I promise that you'll lose them!" Maureen shouted at the man with the pepper spray.

"Um . . . we're sorry," the guard said, letting go of Millie. "We didn't know."

"I tried to tell you stupid muthafuckas that I belong here," Millie snorted. She shambled up to her mother and flashed a yellowing smile. "I made it, Mama. I made it to your party."

"Yes, you did, baby. You did." Maureen fought back tears as she embraced her wayward daughter. The girl smelled like a combination of booze, cigarettes, and funk, but Maureen didn't care. She was just glad to have her child back in her arms.

CHAPTER 22

B ack at the King table, a storm brewed. The more Shadow drank the darker his mood was becoming. Just what Millie warned him against had finally happened—someone snatched his blinders. Thanks to Uncle Chapman, he was finally able to see his family for what they really were.

He cast a glance over at Josette, who hadn't really looked at him since the incident outside. She was still pissed, and rightfully so. When Shadow saw Voodoo, all he could think about was sparing her feelings. He hadn't given much thought to how Josette would feel about being ditched during sex. He had tried to offer a weak apology but she was less than receptive, assuring him without making eye contact that it was her fault and not his. She'd had a lapse in judgment, she said. Her last words to him were, "I thought you were something that you're not." Shadow wasn't sure how to interpret that remark, especially in light of what he had just learned from Chapman.

At the head of the King table, Chance sat beside Orlando, sharing a drink and speaking in hushed tones. Lolli was there next to them in the seat her mother had vacated. She was likely eavesdropping. From the way Chance grinned, whatever he and Orlando were discussing must've been special. But little did the king know that Shadow had planted a fly in the ointment. He wasn't sure if it was the alcohol, or the story that his uncle had disclosed, but he was having a hard time looking at his father. Chancellor King had always been one of Shadow's heroes, a knight in shining armor. Growing up, Shadow was taught that everyone except family was fair game if it inched him closer to his goals. Apparently, though, that rule only applied to those not wearing the crown. When you were the king, you could bend the rules however you saw fit.

"Why you over here glaring at Daddy like you're ready to kill him?" Ghost said, appearing behind Shadow. He placed a hand on his little brother's shoulder.

"I'm good," Shadow grumbled, moving so that Ghost's hand fell away.

Ghost saw that the Zaza women were pretending not to watch Shadow and him. This pissed Ghost off; family business wasn't everybody's business. "Let me talk to you for a second," he said, scooping Shadow under the arm and dragging him from his chair. Ghost found a quiet corner of the hall and shoved his brother into it. "You got something you wanna get off your chest?"

"I told you, I'm good," Shadow said, looking everywhere except at Ghost.

"You're not good. I see you been sitting over here with your face all sour and shit, like somebody did something to you. What happened? Shit didn't go as planned between you and shorty?"

"Went better than it did with you and her sister," Shadow muttered.

"What the fuck did you just say?" Ghost grabbed Shadow by his jacket.

"I know everything, Ghost." The liquor had loosened his lips. "I know what ruined Daddy and Orlando's friendship the first time. That shit was all your fault!"

Ghost was stunned. The one time he failed the family was a secret only a few knew. Someone had obviously clued Shadow in, and from the way Chapman was staring at them from across the room, it didn't take a rocket scientist to figure out who it had been. He would deal with his uncle in due time, but right now he had to come to an understanding with his brother. "Shadow, you don't know the whole story. Let's take a walk and I'll—"

"You'll what? Tell me how this time it'll be different? That this is my responsibly to the family? You might've been willing to let Daddy pawn you off like property to close a business deal, but not me! I am the master of my own destiny. I will choose my own fate!" Shadow stormed away from Ghost.

"What the hell was that all about?" Lolli asked, approaching Ghost.

"Our fucking uncle is stirring the pot, per usual," Ghost fumed. "I'm about to break this nigga's jaw! Maybe that'll help him keep that big-ass mouth closed."

"Ghost, don't start no shit at Mom's party," Lolli called out, chasing after him as he cut across the room toward Chapman.

"I'm going to invite him outside. If he's a man, he'll step out. If he's a bitch, I'm gonna drop him where he stands."

Ghost's anger had reached new heights. Chapman was a troublemaker. He always had been, but for the most part he kept his shenanigans to spreading harmless gossip. But blowing up Ghost's secret to Shadow crossed a line. Ghost had plans to beat Chapman within an inch of his life for what he'd done. Unfortunately, that plan would have to wait. As soon as the brother and sister reached the table, all hell broke loose.

"Chance, one thing about you that hasn't changed over the years is that you still throw the best parties!" Orlando Zaza shouted, slapping Chance on the back before downing yet another glass of champagne. He had consumed at least two bottles on his own, and was obviously feeling good.

"This ain't shit," Chance boasted. "Wait until you attend the shindig I'm going to throw once I'm elected borough president! Ah, Orlando. This will be good for the family—both of our families."

"Right—*all for the family.* Is that how you say it?"

"Yes, and I can't wait to welcome you into ours." Chance raised his glass, but Orlando didn't.

"I'm afraid mine is empty."

"We can't have that!" Chance glanced around and snapped his fingers; a waiter rushed over to fill Orlando's glass. "Leave the bottle," Chance said before dismissing the waiter with a flick of his wrist.

"Must be nice," Orlando said, sipping from his glass, "being able to snap your fingers and people just jump to fulfill whatever your heart desires."

"I'd be lying if I told you that it didn't feel good to be the king," Chance responded. "Speaking of desires of the heart, I took care of that little problem you were having."

Chance was referring to the show of good faith that Orlando had demanded as compensation for getting back into business with him. A situation had popped up that Orlando was having trouble taking care of on his own. A rival Cuban organization had been challenging Orlando's operation in New York and New Jersey by cutting into his gun businesses. The rival, much like Orlando, was connected to some heavyweight old-timers back home, so killing him outright could've started a war. This was where Chance came in. Instead of whacking Orlando's rival, he had him locked up. This was part of the play he had used to leverage Paul Schulman. Some of Chance's boys had paid a visit to the snitch Ira's family, making it clear that if Ira didn't point the finger at the rival instead of Paul, then the king of Five Points would exterminate his whole family.

Ira was instructed to recant the story he'd originally told the feds. Chance would then have the right palms greased to make sure that the prosecutor on the case would accept the bone Chance had tossed him. So long as the prosecutor obtained his conviction, no one would care too much whether the accused was Hebrew or brown. So long as someone went to jail.

"That was quick," Orlando said with a smile.

"When the king speaks, the people listen," Chance capped.

"I'm thankful, but I have to ask: considering our history, who is to say that you won't back out of our arrangement? It wouldn't be the first time you've left me holding my dick."

"I thought you might feel a bit skeptical, which is why I had my people put a rush on all this. By the time we're finished with dessert, the feds should be kicking your problem's door down. He might not be dead, but it'll be at least ten to fifteen years before you have to worry about him again. By then, I'll be in DC and you and your wife will be retired on a beach somewhere while our kids are running our businesses. All that remains now is for you to keep up your end of the bargain and arrange the meeting between me and your folks in Cuba."

"About that . . ." Orlando said. "I don't think it's going to happen."

"What? Why? Did they get cold feet?" Chance was stunned by Orlando's nonchalance. The terms had been agreed to weeks ago and everything should have been set.

"No, I'm sure they'd have been more than willing to sit down with you if I had actually made the call," Orlando said, "which I didn't."

Chance's entire body flooded with rage. "Is this some kind of joke?"

Orlando grinned and slowly shook his head.

"We had a deal," Chance said, punching the table.

"Yes, we did. It's just too bad that I changed my mind. Look, Chance, you're spending so much time rubbing elbows with white people and it's obviously made you take your finger off the pulse of the streets. In our world, all a man has is his word, and once you break that you ain't worth shit. Some years ago, you and your son gave me your word and you broke it. You not only embarrassed me but also my daughter and the Zaza name. It took my wife and me months to try and help my baby piece her heart back together."

"C'mon with this bullshit, Orlando. That shit was foul, I've said as much already and apologized I don't know how many times. I even offered you compensation in the way of my own flesh and blood."

"Yes, young Sean," Orlando said, nodding. "In the short time I've gotten to know him, watch how he moves, I can say that Shadow is a far better man than you or your other piece-of-shit son, Ghost. I see in Sean the potential to truly be great, but he'll likely never reach his full potential so long as his father is pulling the strings of his life. Long story short, if you thought for a minute I would compromise my dignity, or the dignity of my family, and get back into business with the Kings, then obviously the rumors about you going soft in the head and no longer being fit to lead the monarchy have some truth to them."

"You dirty bastard," Chance hissed.

"Look at it like this," Orlando went on, "at least I respected you enough to tell you to your face that I ain't fucking with you, rather than you having to hear it through a third party, like you did to me. That makes us even for your son breaking my baby girl's heart. Charge it to the game . . ."

Orlando continued his gloating, but Chance stopped listening. He was too busy arguing against the voice in his head screaming, *I told you so!* Even Ghost had warned him not to trust

Zaza, yet Chance couldn't see beyond his own political aspirations. He had made promises and called in favors to make this thing happen between he and Orlando, only to find out that his so-called partner had been dealing from the bottom of the deck the whole time. Chance wanted to keep up his noble façade, not regress back to what he really was deep down. Even ignoring Orlando's presence in the room, there were people here who had the power to change lives. People who believed in the man Chance had built himself to be and had forgotten about the man he once was. Appearances were everything in these circles, and the moneymen absolutely shied away from violence. *But you know what?* Chance said to himself. *Fuck all that.*

"Well played, Orlando," he said out loud. "To commemorate your victory, how about we have one last round . . . on you?"

Before Orlando's brain could figure out whether the king was joking or not, Chance was on his feet. He grabbed the bottle the waiter had left at the table and broke it across Orlando's head. He would've stabbed him in the throat with the jagged glass had Ghost not hooked him under the arm and stayed his strike.

"Have you lost your mind?" Ghost whispered in his father's ear. "Remember where we are!"

Seeing the scuffle between their respective leaders, soldiers for both the Kings and the Zazas rose to their feet and a line was drawn in the imaginary sand between them. Lolli, Nefertiti, and Little Stevie formed a protective barrier between Chance and anyone who wasn't a King. Even Millie had managed to sober up enough to realize there was a threat present. Her glassy eyes swept across the Zaza soldiers. She held a steak knife in her tight fish, which she had snatched from one of the dinner plates. Both sides wanted smoke, but neither wanted to light the fire. The tension was immediately so thick that everyone in the room could feel it pushing against them. The guests feared that the prestigious birthday dinner, which they had paid so handsomely to attend, was about to become a ghetto massacre.

When the doors to the hall swung open, the night took yet another unexpected turn.

CHAPTER 23

S hadow shoved open the doors of the banquet hall with so much force that one of them cracked when it bounced off the rubber stopper. He was a ball of rage and needed to get away from the venue.

He wanted to leave as soon as he could. He had ridden with the family in the limo and he knew that there was no way Nefertiti would leave the royal family to drop him off at home. He thought about calling an Uber or Lyft and then remembered that he didn't have his phone; he'd never gotten it back from Josette after their little game. He was about to storm back inside and demand his property when he heard his mother's voice.

"Sean, are you okay?" Maureen had followed him after watching him storm out of the hall.

"I wish everybody would stop asking me that," Shadow spat, pacing back and forth.

Maureen grabbed him by the arm. "I'm your mother. You can talk to me about anything. What's wrong?"

Shadow looked at her. "Did you know? Were you in on this plan to sell me to the Zazas?" Maureen shifted her eyes to the ground. "I should've known," he said, ripping his arm free from her grasp and pacing once again. "Nothing happens in this family without the blessing of the queen. How could you guys even think doing that to Ghost was okay, let alone trying to do it again with me? Didn't you learn the first time that bartering one of your kids would blow up in your fucking faces?"

Maureen seized Shadow by his shoulders, forcing him to stop moving. She delivered two quick slaps across his face. "First of all, watch your mouth. I am your mother, not one of your bitches. Second, before you pass judgment, you need to know the whole story. Sit." She directed him to the rim of a tree potted in a stone cube. She waited until he sat before continuing. "Years ago, we hit a rough patch. Crews were uniting in an attempt to overthrow your father, and it led to war—a war that we very nearly lost. We were backed into a corner and in order to survive, alliances had to be forged. This is where the Zazas came in. Orlando had the muscle and the guns to help turn the tide, but in order to commit to making our problems *his* problems, something stronger than a handshake was required to seal the deal."

"So you pawned off Ghost."

"Ghost was never a pawn. He was a willing participant, at least in the beginning. He was already banging Orlando's daughter behind our backs, so he was halfway there anyhow. I can't say that he was totally thrilled about the prospect of marrying a girl he didn't know that well, but if it ensured the survival of our family, then Ghost was willing to do it. He understood the importance of making sacrifices, not like some of my more self-centered children."

Shadow didn't respond.

"The marriage between Carmen Zaza and Ghost was supposed to bind our two families in name and blood, making us stronger than ever. When the time came, Ghost would ascend to the throne and hold command over the Zaza army. My boy would've been the strongest king that Five Points had ever seen."

"Then what happened?" Shadow asked, his anger subsiding.

"Ghost fell in love," Maureen sighed. "While most of us

were occupied with planning the wedding, Ghost made plans of his own with Kelly. I tried to get that fool boy to forget about her, to look at the bigger picture. Carmen Zaza brought a pedigree and influence. What did Kelly bring to the table besides a GED and a wet pussy? She was hardly good enough for my C.J., but the heart wanted what the heart wanted. I knew Kelly would be trouble from the first time I laid eyes on her, but I had no idea the level of destruction she'd bring to my boy's head."

"I guess the Zazas didn't take it well, him having another chick on the side?"

"To the contrary. I don't think anyone would've cared if Ghost kept the girl as a mistress, like I suggested he do. Most married men have sidepieces. Even your dad had a few in the beginning of our marriage. Kelly wouldn't hear it though. She wanted all of Ghost or none of him. It was her ultimatum that made my son jump out the window headfirst and burn down everything we had been trying to build. It happened at the engagement party, which we never even told you about. I'd been having a bad feeling that entire day and it didn't help that Ghost showed up an hour late. He stood up in front of all those people and announced that he couldn't go through with the marriage because his heart belonged to someone else. Carmen Zaza had never been one of my favorite people, but that night I felt truly bad for her. She was so embarrassed that she cried until she had an asthma attack. The only reason Orlando didn't try and kill Ghost is because he didn't want a war with the monarchy. Still, things changed between him and your dad after that."

"And so you guys trying to hook me up with Josette Zaza was your way of restoring the peace between the two families?" Shadow still didn't like the move, but he understood it a little better.

"In a sense. But plugging you in with the Zaza family was supposed to work more to your benefit than anyone else's."

"How so?"

"I love all my children, but I'm afraid of what your father handing the monarchy over to Ghost will do."

"You think Ghost wouldn't make a good king?"

"Only time will tell. I know he'll do his best, but Ghost is not a leader of men like your father, or even you."

"Me?"

"Sean, I see such greatness in you. You are smart, kind, and honest. When you finally stop being so lazy and recognize your full potential, you'll go on to do amazing things. But that will never happen so long as you live in the shadow of your brother and this monarchy. Becoming the head of the Zaza family would not only establish you as a king in your own right, but it would protect us in the unlikely event that things go south with Ghost on the throne. Two kings in the family gives us better odds at survival."

All Shadow could do was stare at his mother in awe. He knew that she could be a cagey old bird, but until then he had no idea exactly how calculating she was. Leave it to Maureen King to have a plan within a plan. He was about to apologize to her for his behavior and promise that he would at least consider her proposition, but their conversation was broken up by the screeching of car tires.

Two unmarked vehicles rolled up the driveway of the banquet hall, followed by several blue-and-white cars. A dozen cops filed out and bull-rushed their way inside the banquet hall.

"What's going on?" Shadow gasped.

"What the fuck is this?" Little Stevie asked, looking at the sea of cops flooding the space.

"Trouble," Lolli replied. She stashed her gun in an ice bucket on the table and backed away from it.

Chippie rushed across the room and blocked the path of the cops. "I'm sorry, but this is a private party. Invitation only."

"Consider this our invitation," said a sloppily dressed white detective, who slid an arrest warrant into Chippie's hand before brushing past her and heading for the royal family's table.

As Ghost watched the detectives move in his direction, his stomach churned. One of them twirled a pair of handcuffs around his finger, smirking like a child. Ghost's eyes darted around, trying to locate the nearest exit. It was no use; the police had the whole place locked down. He was trapped. His thoughts turned to the conversation he'd had with Monster about the cops having a witness to the Freddy hit. He had been both careless and stupid for doing the hit himself instead of using one of his soldiers. He'd suspected that one day karma would catch up with him, but not so soon and not like this. He hadn't even had his chance in the big chair yet.

Ghost gazed at his stone-faced and stoic father, who appeared to have no idea what was happening. Even if he did, he was the king and had to maintain an appearance of control at all times, especially amid chaos.

Lolli was now sweating through her dress like a hooker in church. The Zazas watched in what looked like amused anticipation. It pained Ghost to know that they would be happy watching him walk out of the hall in handcuffs, a just payback for what he'd done to their daughter. But if they were expecting a show, they wouldn't get one. Ghost was a G and he would take this on the chin like he did everything else. With his chest out and his chin high, he stepped in front of the detective and extended his wrist. *All for the family,* he assured himself while awaiting the cold bite of the iron bracelets. To his surprise, the detective hardly gave him a second look, moving straight past him.

"Chancellor King?" the sloppy-looking detective said, sizing up the king of Five Points.

"Fuck y'all pigs doing here, busting up my wife's party?" Chance capped. "Didn't you get your donation this month?"

"You're a funny guy," the detective said, "but let's see how funny you find this warrant for your arrest." He twirled the handcuffs once more for good measure.

"For what?" Chance asked with a small grin. The closest he had come to personally breaking the law in the last ten years was the ass whipping he had just put on Orlando Zaza, and it wasn't likely that the man had called it in.

"Racketeering, murder, and conspiracy to commit murder," the detective recited before shoving Chance against the table and folding one of his arms behind his back.

"This is some bullshit! Who am I supposed to have killed?" The racketeering charge he was sure he could get his lawyer to make go away—maybe even the conspiracy—but the murder allegation concerned him. He couldn't even remember the last time he had taken a life.

"The name Alderman James Porter ring a bell?" the detective asked.

"Get the fuck out of here! Me and James are friends. Why would I kill him?" There were a number of people who wouldn't have minded seeing the alderman dead, but Chance wasn't one of them.

"This is a mistake!" Lolli yelled, slipping in front of the detective.

"Ma'am, I'm going to need you to step back!" the detective barked, extending his arm to keep distance between them.

"Don't worry, honey," Chance said, "we're going to get this all sorted out."

"But you don't understand." Tears welled in Lolli's eyes. "It wasn't my father who killed Alderman Porter!"

It took a second for it to click in Chance's head what Lolli was insinuating. She couldn't have—could she? "Ghost, get your sister out of here! Now!" he commanded.

Ghost was reluctant to leave his father, but the urgency in his voice couldn't be ignored. He grabbed Lolli by the arm and started pulling her toward the exit.

"No . . . I can't let Daddy go down for this! I can't!" Lolli yelled, but Ghost was too strong.

Maureen and Shadow reentered the hall just as the police were escorting Chance from the table. Maureen's heart leaped from her chest and she brought her hands to her face. Before she went outside, everything had been fine—what had happened? How could it all have gone to shit so quickly?

"Chance!" she called out to her husband.

"Don't worry, baby," Chance responded over his shoulder. "This ain't about nothing. Have Chippie get the lawyer on the line."

Shadow watched as the police loaded the king into a squad car and slammed the door behind him. Ghost stood off to the side trying to console Lolli, who was going to pieces. Shadow felt a presence behind him, followed by a hand placed on his shoulder—Uncle Chapman.

"Heavy is the head that wears the crown," Chapman whispered.

Shadow looked at his uncle. It was like he had stepped out of his body and was now watching himself from the sidelines. He drew back and slugged his uncle in the mouth with everything he had. Blood burst from Chapman's lip and splashed on Shadow's white shirt. He was about to sock him again, when a pair of strong hands grabbed him from behind and pulled him back inside the banquet hall.

"Boy, have you lost your damn mind? You can't be swinging on people all crazy in front of the police!" Little Stevie scolded.

"Fuck the police and fuck that bitch-ass uncle of mine. He's lucky I didn't kill him!"

"Yeah, you kill him and you'll be in a cell next to your daddy instead of where you belong, which is out here with us trying to figure out what's going down."

"My dad didn't kill anybody," Shadow declared.

"Whether he did or didn't isn't the issue right now," Stevie told him. "Who put the finger on him is. I need you to pull yourself together so you can help Ghost get the women straight while I do some digging and see if I can find out what's happening. Do you think you can do that?"

Shadow nodded.

"Good. Go keep your head up and your mouth closed. I'll reach out to you and Ghost when I know something," Stevie said before disappearing into the night.

Shadow parked himself on a chair outside the dining room of the banquet hall. The guests filed out, everyone murmuring about what had just happened to Chance and what it would mean. Some of them stopped and tried to offer Shadow words of kindness, but he couldn't hear anything but his heart thudding in his ears. Someone sought to destroy his family. When he found out who that was, he would make them answer for it.

Shadow finally stood and was about to join his family at the limo so they could head home. There was nothing else to be done at the banquet hall. Yet as he stalked off, something on the floor caught his eye. It was the envelope Juliette Zaza had given his mother earlier that night. *A little something on your special day to show how much love and respect we have for the Kings,* she had said. Out of curiosity more than anything else, Shadow opened the envelope. Inside it was a single dollar bill.

EPILOGUE

Two weeks had passed since Chance's arrest and things had only gone further downhill. The judge denied him bail, stating that his finances and political connections made him a flight risk. His lawyer appealed the ruling, but the situation appeared grim.

The media relished dragging Chancellor King's name through the mud and a great many of his so-called friends distanced themselves from him. Men who he had been doing legitimate business with for years now wouldn't touch him with a ten-foot pole. Being associated with someone facing such serious charges was bad for business. Even the council of lords within the monarchy kept their distance. They claimed that Chance was hot and they didn't want to bring any unnecessary heat to the monarchy.

Lolli had come clean to Ghost about why she'd broken down when Chance was arrested. Unbeknownst to everyone except Nefertiti, she had met with Alderman Porter about supporting her father, but he had rudely dismissed her. This hadn't sat right with Lolli, so she went back for another visit. This time, the conversation was held over the business end of her gun. They had exchanged words and she had thrown him a good beating, but Lolli insisted that he was still alive when she'd left him. The fight was the source of the blood on her clothes that Shadow caught her trying to hide. The alderman's maid had identified Lolli's vehicle from when she was there earlier, a vehicle registered in the name of Chancellor King. This explained how the police caught the trail. Lolli was many things, but a liar wasn't one of them. If she said she didn't kill Porter then she didn't, but that raised the question as to who did and what they stood to gain by placing the blame on Chance. The rabbit hole would go even deeper when Ghost finally went to visit his father in the lockup.

The conversation between the father and son was short and to the point. They still had no clue who had put the murder charge on Chance, yet the conspiracy to commit murder could've only come from one person. Chance had told Ghost about the agreement he struck with Paul Schulman. The thing that Chance had asked of Paul in exchange for making the Ira problem go away was to take a life. Not just any life, but the life of Dickey Salvatore. Chance understood that there would be some pushback, and that it would be challenging to figure out who was next in line to lead the Salvatore family. But if Dickey wasn't around to pressure the monarchy into turning against Chance for his career decision, the transition would be smoother. Chance waited until after he visited with Rocco before pushing the button on the hit. He could tell from the lack of respect shown to him by Dickey that, eventually, one of them would probably have to die. The only two people who knew about Chance's contingency plan were himself and Paul. That had to be where the conspiracy came from. For his betrayal, Chance planned to have Paul and several of his goons wiped off the map. And there was only one person he could trust with this delicate task.

For the rest of the day, Ghost replayed the conversation he'd had with his father over and over again. The old man was in bad shape, more rattled than Ghost had ever seen him.

Chance was usually so confident, adept at talking or buying his way out of any situation. But this time the feds had him by the balls. Ghost knew this when his father tasked him with the job of getting rid of Paul Schulman. Knocking Paul and a few key associates out would likely make the conspiracy go away, and from there they could work on the murder beef. It would be one less thing hanging over his head. This was the only time Chance had ever asked Ghost to kill. And this is how Ghost fully comprehended how desperate his father truly was.

Because of everything going on, Ghost had a good amount of heat on him too, but he would not deny his father's request.

"You don't have to be here," Monster said. "You know that, don't you?"

"Nah, I gotta do this," Ghost told him. "Dad was specific that it had to be me."

They rode through Williamsburg in a stolen Cutlass, dressed in all black. "I'll take care of this shit for you. I don't even know why Uncle Chance didn't just come to me. You guys know that I've always been willing to do anything for this family, including push a nigga's wig back."

"I know, Monster. You've always been a good soldier." Ghost thought of the territory he had planned to gift Monster. With everything going on, he hadn't had a chance to tell him yet.

"That's the thing," Monster said. "I've been a good soldier for a little too long. I've seen guys come into the family after me, pass me by, and I'm still in the streets busting heads. Maybe it's time that Uncle Chance opens the books and makes me a full member. I think I'm owed at least that."

"*Owed?* Nigga, nobody owes you nothing. We all earn our way around here," Ghost shot back, his mood instantly souring.

"And I ain't been earning my way? How many suckas have

I wasted for you, Ghost? While you sit in the big house getting fat, I'm in the streets putting the fear of God in these niggas. It hurts when I keep getting passed over. That's all I'm saying."

Ghost sighed. "Look, man, after I take care of this piece of business, we can have a long conversation about exactly what it is you're owed. Until then, shut the fuck up, drive the car, and let me concentrate."

Monster scowled before turning his attention back to the road. Paul had been MIA since Chance had gotten arrested, but they had received a tip that afternoon that he had a meeting scheduled with his uncle Benjamin at Morning Star Meats. This was their best and probably last chance to catch Paul before he went back underground. They were a few blocks from Morning Star when Monster pulled the car over in front of a bodega and killed the engine.

"We got shit to do, man," Ghost said. "We ain't got time for no snacks." Sometimes it seemed like all Monster knew how to do was eat and hurt people.

"I'm out of smokes," Monster said, balling up an empty pack of cigarettes and tossing it out the window. "I'll only be a second. You need anything?"

"I need you to hurry the fuck up so I can put in this work and get back to the house and put my father's affairs in order!"

Monster ignored him and got out of the car. He was really starting to work Ghost's nerves. Maybe he shouldn't bump him up after all. That might be letting a bull loose in a china shop. Still, he would have to do something to appease the big man or risk putting more distance between them. The way things were shaping up, he would need every able-bodied killer he knew at his disposal. If war was a possibility, he would be ready.

As Ghost reclined in the passenger seat, lost in his thoughts, he spotted a flicker of motion through one of the side mirrors.

Someone was creeping up alongside the car. Swiftly, Ghost reached under the seat and retrieved his gun. Whoever was moving against him was about to be in for a rude awakening. Ghost waited until the man reached the passenger door, preparing to throw it open and spring. It was locked. He tried the release, but nothing happened. Someone had put the child locks on. A bullet shattered the window, hitting Ghost in his collar. When he turned to crawl into the driver's seat, a second bullet hit him in the back. Fighting through the pain, Ghost managed to lower himself into the driver's seat. He needed to get out of the car. When he went to put the vehicle in drive, he realized two things: Monster had taken the key, and there was more than one assailant.

The shooters pumped round after round into the car, tearing Ghost up. Although he couldn't hear himself, he knew he was screaming because his mouth was open and his vocal cords strained in pain. The door finally opened and Ghost spilled out onto the curb. He grabbed the car door and tried to pull himself to his feet. Even the five or six bullets lodged in his body hadn't taken all the fight out of him. Blood pooled in his eyes, making it hard to see, but he recognized Judah standing before him, holding a pistol. The other dude was Cheese.

"Talk that shit now, bitch-ass nigga!" Cheese shouted, striking Ghost in the side of the head with his gun.

Ghost lay on the pavement, bleeding out. His breathing was labored and he couldn't feel his arms or legs. Cheese and Judah stood over him, and Ghost knew the end was near. He prayed for a miracle.

His prayer was answered when his eyes landed on Monster, who had exited bodega. He was tapping a pack of cigarettes on the back of his hand. "I might be dying," Ghost croaked, "but I'll have some company for the ride." Yes, Monster would avenge him. Ghost waited for his cousin to waste the youngsters . . . but he didn't. He just stood there, smoking his cigarette and watching his cousin bleed. "Monster?" Ghost groaned.

"I told you it was a mistake to not let me kill them," Monster said, taking a long drag from his cigarette.

"Why?" Ghost rasped.

"You lost your way, Cousin," Monster answered. "The reason your soldiers always loved you was because you were one of us. Somewhere along the line, though, you started to forget the people who put you in power. Treated us like we were lesser than you or not as smart as you. I guess we ain't as dumb as you thought."

"Traitor!" Ghost wheezed, spitting blood on Monster's boot.

"Better a traitor than a savage," Monster replied. "That kid you were pressing me to kill? I paid his mother off a week ago to disappear back to whatever third world country they came from. I fed you the information about the witness to see exactly how far out in the deep end you were. They may call me Monster, but it's you who's the real monster." He paused, holding back a swell of anger. Ghost couldn't tell if his cousin was crying or not. "Uncle Chance was right about it being time for a new king, but he was wrong about it being you. Somebody needs to sit on that throne who sees the bigger picture. Someone who will put the needs of this family above their own ego. I love this family, Ghost, which is why I have to be the one to save it. All for the family, right?"

"I'll see you in hell," Ghost said through gritted teeth.

"Maybe, but not no time soon." Monster gave Judah and Cheese the nod to finish the job and stood back.

The youngsters emptied their clips into Ghost's body. When the shells were spent, Cheese pulled out a knife and slit Ghost's throat. A part of Monster felt bad about doing his cousin like this, but it didn't seem as if there was any other way forward. Uncle Chance was about to ruin the monarchy by handing the crown to Ghost, so after careful consideration, Monster had thrown his support behind someone he felt was better equipped to run the monarchy. Someone who would recognize how valuable Monster could be to the family. He was tired of being a foot soldier. He needed a seat at the table. With that in mind, he pulled out his phone and made a call.

Maureen was tired—body and soul. She'd been on the phone with Chance's lawyers all week, and when she wasn't on the phone she was running all across town seeking help wherever she could get it. As expected, many had turned their backs on the king. In the game they played, you were only as good as what you could do for someone. At that moment, Chance couldn't do anything for anyone, not even for himself. Maureen's family was falling apart and she felt powerless to do anything to stop it. Still, she had to press on.

As she made her way down the hall to her bedroom, she thought she heard a voice coming from Chance's office. She placed her ear to the door and there was indeed someone inside her husband's sanctum. She pushed the door open and found Chapman sitting behind Chance's desk, talking on his cell phone. When he saw Maureen, he jumped like he had been caught with his hand in the cookie jar.

"What are you doing in here?" Maureen asked.

"I'm sorry. I needed a phone number from Chance's Rolodex," Chapman said. "I've got an angle that I'm working to try and get his case in front of another judge. Maybe this one will cut us some slack on his bail."

"I sure hope so. Well, you know Chance don't like nobody in his private space."

"I know and I'll be going as soon as I'm done with this call."

Maureen stood there for a moment longer, trying to read Chapman's thoughts. She mumbled something under her breath before turning and leaving.

Chapman waited until he was sure that she was gone before continuing his call.

"The girl might present a problem, but not the son. The boy is a pussy and ain't got it in him. Now is not a good time, but we'll speak face-to-face tomorrow. *Shalom*."

Just when Chapman thought his day couldn't get any better, it did just that. He bounced up and down in the chair like a child who had just been gifted his favorite snack. It wouldn't be long now. His eyes drifted to the display case on the far wall that contained the prizes of the King children: Ghost's boxing trophies, Shadow's football awards, Lolli's martial arts ribbons. Yet the pride of the display case was the golden crown. It was a ceremonial piece that had been in the King family for several generations, even before the formation of the monarchy.

Chapman stared at his reflection in the case. The crown was level with his head, giving him the impression that he was wearing it. He smiled at his reflection and whispered, "Long live the king."

TO BE CONTINUED . . .

9 781636 140148